STILL WRAPPED IN *Obsession*

TASH

Contents

Dedication

To all the women who have been loved with a kind of obsession that outlives time,
and when you returned to their orbit, they never let you go.

Translations

Here is a list of translations to help you through some of the different languages throughout the story.

Anata = You (informal/intimate, Japanese)

Yume = Dream (Japanese)

Lykáki = She-wolf (Greek)

Primo = Cousin (male) (Spanish)

Hai = Yes (Japanese)

Shiru beki datta = I should have known (Japanese)

Hallo = Hello (German)

Μαμά = Mom / Mama (Greek)

Si = Yes (Spanish)

Esta es la familia de mi madre = This is my mother's family (Spanish)

Otōsan = Dad / Father (Japanese)

Hijo = Son (Spanish)

Te quiero, Mama, te quiero = I love you, Mom, I love you (Spanish)

Tuviste algo que ver con que se llevaran a mis hijos = Did you have anything to do with them taking my children? (Spanish)

Mis nietos = My grandchildren (Spanish)

Jefa = Boss (female) / Chief (Spanish)

Me entiendes, carajo = Do you understand me, damn it? (Spanish)

Pero = But (Spanish)

Hermano = Brother (Spanish)

Taiyo-chan = Taiyo (name) + "chan" (cute/affectionate honorific in Japanese)

Otōchan = Dad / Daddy (more affectionate than otōsan) (Japanese)

Mis hijas = My daughters (Spanish)

Kuso = Damn / Shit (Japanese)

Moró mou = (This looks misspelled/unclear; I can't translate reliably without context)

Señor = Sir / Mister (Spanish)

Quiénes son = Who are they? (Spanish)

Soy tu papa = I'm your dad (Spanish)

Contéstame = Answer me (Spanish)

Gracias, querida = Thank you, dear (Spanish)

Cafecito = Little coffee / coffee (often Cuban/Latino style) (Spanish)

Los siento = I'm sorry (Spanish)

pan de yucas = yucca bread (Spanish)

Listo = Ready / Done (Spanish)

Kumichō = Yakuza boss (Japanese)

Oyabun = Boss (yakuza leader) (Japanese)

Magotachis = Grandchildren (Japanese, affectionate pluralized form)

Aguanta = Hold on / Wait (Spanish)

Gordito = Chubby / little chubby one (term of endearment) (Spanish)

Oniichan = Big brother (affectionate) (Japanese)

Author's Note

First off! No matter how you found me, thank you for giving my book baby some love. There are a few things I need you to know before you go diving headfirst into this book.

After you read this and you decide to continue, I don't want to hear shit about anything because that's what this note's for... So, we on the same page now? Okay.

Still Wrapped in Obsession is a continuation from the novella from last year, **Wrapped in Obsession**. Meaning, you are about to jump right into an already going story. Also, these characters and others have been mentioned before in my first book, **Take Me There.** You don't have to read it in order to understand what is going on in here, but some things will make more sense... The stories aren't exactly connected but of the same world.. you get me? Okay, cool.. hmmm.. oh yeah, While this book takes place around Christmas doesn't mean its a Christmas book.... think... Die Hard lol. Okay let me give y'all trigger-warning happy heauxs the list so y'all know what you wanna read... hahaha iykyk.

Happy reading, and enjoy as Carter, G, and Lorelei navigate the situation they are currently in and then find their way back to the obsessive bubble they yearn for..

xoxo Tash

Trigger Warnings

Hi my babies! Just like the first book your mental health is of upmost importance. Even though y'all know the vibes of dark contemporary books, I just want to give y'all a bit of a heads up to what y'all may find in here.

Violence and killing
Gun violence and shootouts
Blood and injury
Kidnapping and captivity
Child endangerment and trafficking themes
Threats, intimidation, and coercive control
Family trauma
MFM / Why Choose
Explicit sexual content
Restraint and power exchange (consensual)
References to sexual assault and forced marriage (backstory)
Strong language
Trauma responses and panic

Lorelei

After the twins' kidnapping...

I stood in the middle of the walk-in shower, water hitting me from every direction. If I weren't so numb, I might've appreciated the pressure — how it poured down perfectly, washing everything clean.

But I couldn't.

There wasn't a single piece of me left that could even muster up a fuck to give.

My babies were gone.

Just hours ago, I'd kissed their little heads, promising cookies and hot chocolate when I got home.

Now I didn't even know where they were.

Steam built up around me, and I just stood there staring off into space. I couldn't hear anything outside of the shower, but I knew that life still breathed in this house. Hell, I just helped Faven give birth to two sweet little humans.

But even *that* couldn't bring me solace right now.

The cries of my babies, knowing that Wolfe was being the best brother he always was to Dream, most likely calming her, was all I could hear.

I needed to wash my body, but I didn't even have it in me to lift my hand to reach for the loofah Carter left for me.

All I could do was stare at the blue tiled wall across from me, hoping, wishing that it morphed into the glassed mosaic that was in my bathroom at home. That all this shit was a dream and my babies weren't in the wind with a fucking unknown psychopath.

I hadn't uttered a word since G and Carter were able to calm me down. My sobs and guttural screams still rang in my ears.

Everything about this was wrong.

Seeing both of them was wrong. This wasn't my life.

I had left that all behind when I moved back home from Aurora. Well, not really home to Syracuse, but to Ithaca.

Why did I choose that? I didn't know. Something pulled me here, and learning that they had been here must have been the reason why.

I heard the creak of the door from someone opening it, but I still couldn't move. The shower door opened, and the warm jasmine scent let me know it was my sister.

"Lo," she called me, but again, I didn't move. I just stood there. "You have to get out the shower."

Still, no words... no movement.

One blink, two.

But nothing more.

My sister sighed heavily before reaching into the shower and turning the water off. She must have had a towel already in her arms because she wrapped me in it moments after the pellets of water stopped beating on my skin.

She took my hand and attempted to pull me out, but I couldn't even get my legs to move.

"Dammit, Lo," she fussed. "You have to give me something, girl."

What was there to give her really? The twins were my everything. They were my very reason for existing, and without them, I felt empty.

My world felt empty not hearing the little pattering of their feet, the giggles as they chased each other, the endless amount of times they called 'Mama' in a day. I was empty.

I finally understood how Bella Swan felt when Edward left her and she spent six months basically just existing.

That was a perfect depiction of how I felt right now.

The air in the bathroom shifted, and for the first time since I stepped foot in the shower, I moved. Turning, I came face to face with hazel orbs that hurt to look into. Wolfe had the exact same eyes as his.

"I got her." That unique accent I'd only heard from him filled my ears, and the dam broke.

I crumbled right there staring into his addictive eyes.

My cries must have been loud enough to alert his other half because he came barreling into the bathroom. His large imposing frame dwarfed the space instantly.

Like a moth to a flame, our eyes met, and the storm they pulled me in was just like Dream's, and if possible, my screams became louder... more gut wrenching.

"Yume."

"Lykáki."

They spoke at the same time. Their meanings made me cry harder.

I wonder if they knew their names. If they knew I tried my best to honor them in their lives. To tell them the fairytale version of how two dark knights saved the women and turned her world upside down for the best.

How I told Wolfe his quiet strength was earned from his father, and to Dream, that her ability to adapt came from hers.

There weren't pictures to reference, but I made sure they knew that if their fathers knew of them they would be there.

Now I don't know if any of them would ever get the chance to experience each other and that. That was what broke me the most.

Carter bent down and scooped me into his arms carrying me back into the bedroom we now occupied. G was right by his side, his large hand running through my drenched locs.

Quietly, my sister followed. Silent tears streamed down her face. I wanted to comfort her because she loved my kids as if they were hers, and vice versa. But how could I comfort her when I could barely breathe myself?

"Deidra said she had something she could wear," my sister said as she walked to the door leading out of the room. "I'll be right back."

"I have a shirt for her," G spoke stoically.

Carter sat me on the bed, and again, my cries were gone, but I was stuck in the loop of not moving.

"In that case, I can stay and dress her," my sister voiced.

I could tell by her tone she wanted them to leave me because my sudden outburst happened the moment they entered the room. And if I had the ability, I would tell her that I wanted, no, *needed* them in here and honestly needed her to go.

"We have it, Solelei," Carter told her sternly.

Silence fell. I did not have to look to know the weight of the stare they were giving her. I did not know everything about Carter and G, but I knew enough. They radiated danger.

"Okay, and?" Solelei sassed. "I don't know why the both of you have been drawn to my sister, but I draw the line at y'all dressing."

"Lei," I barely whispered. "I am okay. They..." I looked up to the men who had a hand in giving me the world. "They're Dream and Wolfe's dads."

My sister's head snapped to me. "They're the twins, what?" she gasped. "B... but I thought you didn't know who the father was, and you're telling me there are two?"

I cleared my throat attempting to free it from the complex emotions that had thickened there. She wasn't wrong in her assumption, but it was just that... an assumption.

Whenever asked, I never gave an answer to the paternity of the twins. How the fuck was I supposed to explain to anyone that two men kidnapped me four years ago on Christmas, and I not only slept with them but at the same time? And that one time, even with many rounds, produced two kids that were twins, but the only thing they shared was my DNA.

There was no need to have a test done. My children's eyes told me everything I needed to know in regard to their paternity.

"Yes, Lei," I blandly stated, still not wanting to explain but not for the reasons I had previously. I just didn't have the shit in me to be honest.

"Wow!" I could hear the judgment in her voice, but again, I didn't have it in me to give a damn. "Regardless, they couldn't bother being there past busting a nut, so again, I am going to have to ask both of you to leave."

Gerasimou chuckled darkly. I knew right then if I didn't get Solelei out of this room, it wasn't going to end well, and I *really* didn't have the capacity for it.

I truly felt like a fucking broken record.

"Solelei!" I barked at her. She gave me an incredulous look, almost like she was shocked and appalled that I seemingly was taking the side of two strangers over her. The thing was, they weren't strangers.

Sure, I didn't know much about them or that I hadn't seen them since technically Christmas morning four years ago. However, our souls... our souls knew each other.

The connection we shared was something that couldn't be explained, but I felt it. Its potency so strong that the universe saw it fit to have them leave their mark with me creating two perfect little humans.

"You know the fuck what," she hissed. "Let me get my ass out of here before I say something that I can't come back from." With that, she stormed out.

The room fell back to silence as Gerasimou produced a shirt that he put over my head. Carter used a microfiber towel to dry my locs. After getting the majority of the water out, he went into the bathroom and came out with a blow dryer.

He blow dried my hair until it was dry enough that it wouldn't wet the bed. Gerasimou then put my locs into a high bun and placed a large bonnet over them.

They both climbed into the bed behind me and pulled me in their embrace. A place I had dreamed and silently yearned to be for so long.

As they held me, my mind simultaneously calmed but ran, trying to figure out how I was going to get my babies back.

I felt like a failure that I left my babies vulnerable to be taken.

"I'm sorry," I whispered into his chest. It was muffled, but him pulling me close let me know he still heard me.

"No, *yume-chan*, I'm sorry." He sounded pained, and it gutted me.

Pulling my head back, I locked eyes with him, his hazel eyes held so much pain. And guilt. I turned quickly to lock eyes with Gerasimou, and his eyes, too, held the same pain as Carter's.

"You know who took them, don't you?" I asked Carter, but I knew the answer. I remembered hearing Carter saying *primo* to the man who called from Celeste's phone.

"*Hai,*" he answered.

I pulled my bottom lip in with my teeth. A part of me wanted to go off, but they were apparently tied into the Sivad Syndicate somehow, something I wished that I knew before I chose to lay with them.

Not me acting like I had a choice.

Having knowledge of that actually gave me hope. I knew how the Sivad was and what they were capable of. I might have been estranged from them, but I was raised within its organization.

If there was anyone who could find my babies before anything happened to them, it would be the most feared and respected Syndicate in the world.

Still, even though I trusted that they would stop at nothing to get our babies back, I needed some space to breathe.

Moving to sit up between them, I somehow was able to hold both of their stares. We sat like that watching each other and allowing the tangible grief we all felt, to fill the silence.

The longer we sat staring at each other the more the grief began to morph into need. Desire.

For the last four years, I had been trying my best to not be in this mental headspace where I needed them, where I craved their presence. Their touches, kisses, *love*.

Yes, love. Time wasn't needed for me to feel and know that they loved me. For a while, I thought I imagined my feelings whenever I thought about our time together, but being here crowded by them, I could confidently say what we shared was very real.

My body heated as they continued to stare at me, and dammit if I didn't want them, no, if I didn't need them to do something that made everything I was feeling to stop. Even if it was only for a moment.

I hadn't been with anyone since them, and it wasn't for lack of trying. But not a single man could measure up to the feeling they gave me.

Hell, I shouldn't even be thinking about it at a time like this.

The soft glow of light given by the sconces built into the headboard gave me just enough light to be able to see them clearly. Carter's hazel eyes looked at me with a mix between wonderment and infatuation. Gerasimou's stormy gray eyes looked at me as if I even thought to give him a green light to consume me; he would do so with no hesitation, leaving nothing behind.

"*Yume...*"

"*Lykáki...*"

They both spoke at the same time again. This time they said it in a tone that did something to my body.

Fuck, it did everything to my soul.

They were studying me hard. Normally, anyone staring at me for that long would make me feel exposed. But under their scrutiny, I felt alive. I was captive to them and stripped of everything only to be built back up in their image, and I'd be damned if I didn't rise to the occasion.

Without words, without prompting, they advanced on me. In sync, in tandem. So fucking effortlessly you would think we'd done this dance more than the one and only time my body felt so alive.

Gerasimou kissed the right side of my neck, nuzzling his nose into the crook of my neck. Kissing, sucking, and licking it like it was the ice cream that melted.

Carter went for my mouth. I expected it to be a soft, loving kiss, but this man took possession of my mouth like I held the answers to the universe between my back molars.

The sensory overload was everything, and while a voice in the back of my mind was telling me I needed to stop this to put the focus back on finding our missing children, my body wouldn't allow me to.

They switched off with each other, Carter now peppering kisses down the column of my neck and Gerasimou devouring my lips. They alternated with each other, bringing my body to the brink. I was so fucking turned on, my lower region thudded. My head felt like I was floating, and the sound of their lips smacking on different parts of my skin sent all my blood to the places they touched.

Just as quickly as they started, they both pulled away from me. The rapid beating of my heart and our in-sync shallow breathing was all that could be heard.

Frustration bloomed in my chest. Not only was I distraught, but the very thing they could do to take my mind from it, they denied me of.

"Not now, *Yume*," Carter said as he pulled me into their embrace, which made the thudding of my middle worse.

Gerasimou kissed my forehead. "We want you the same. But we don't deserve the reward of you until we return our babies to you."

They laid us down in a way to others that might not seem practical, but it worked so damn well for us.

As we held onto each other, my heart filled with contentment and emptiness at the same time.

Gerasimou

"I named them Wolfe and Dream," she spoke lowly.

We were still in the bed, Lykáki lying between us, pressed close. That brief taste of her lips and skin still lingered on my lips. Silence hung heavy, and I welcomed it. I needed it, needed to sort through the storm in my chest.

Less than twelve fucking hours ago, I came face to face with the woman who had haunted every dream I'd had whenever sleep came, and every thought when I was elbows deep in sending someone to the maker.

When Carter and I agreed to get the midwife, we never expected it would be her. *My Lykáki.*

We had Scott monitoring her since we left. Any reason to step in, we were supposed to be notified. How did her carrying our goddamn children not set off Carter's four-eyed ass? The answer to that question wasn't necessary.

When that dead man walking spat that twins-of-the-same-mother-not-father bullshit, I brushed it off at first, thinking he was trying to get a rise out of me. It wasn't until she confirmed it with her sister; although, if I was being real, I already felt it in my blood. One of them belonged to me.

"Did you say something, Yume?" Carter's voice cut through. He heard her too. But I needed it again.

"I named the twins Wolfe and Dream. Even before they were born. The moment the doctor told me their genders, I knew what their names would be."

"*Yume.*"

"*Lykáki.*"

"Mhm," she murmured, nestling closer between us.

The three of us pressed together tighter in the bed at her revelation. We were tight enough I knew if Banks walked in, he'd start spewing that gay bullshit about Carter and me. I'd let him because I never gave a fuck about correcting a motherfucker on a thing.

People were going to think what they wanted. What no one knew or wouldn't understand was that I owed Carter my life. Since that moment he helped me, we were inseparable. Even during my time living with the *Iron Saints* and his in Japan, we were in sync.

Lykáki moved, stretched, then climbed out of the bed toward the bathroom. I followed her with my eyes. I couldn't look away even if I wanted to. The shirt I gave her barely covered her ass, and fuck, I remembered every curve, every freckle, every dip...

Clothed like this, they were the same but slightly altered, expanded by carrying life. No one would guess she'd birthed twins. Her thighs spread, her breasts fuller. My mouth went dry. Every ounce of willpower went into not stripping her bare, into not taking what my body had been screaming for all over again.

Four years. Four years I'd carried the memory of Carter and I owning her mind, body, and soul. Walking away that night? Hardest thing I'd ever done.

Knowing she woke up that morning alone and terrified, tore me apart every day. Knowing she carried our children, raised them alone, sharpened the guilt I still felt.

At the time, leaving was the right choice. Henrik called. Norway first, then Ithaca. Shit with the Sivad and Faven became our new priority, and there was never a moment we could come for her like we wanted. Leaving us no choice but to neglect the need we had.

Our negligence put her and the twins at risk. That's the price we paid.

But if there was one thing I knew for sure, my heart belonged to Lorelei Rose Kincaid. Carter was the same. We'd get our children back. Whole. Without a scratch.

The sound of the toilet flushing, the sink running, pulled me from the dark, murderous thoughts I felt coming.

She stepped out.

Fuck.

She stole the air from the room. Sadness still clung to her eyes, but something else was there too. Her warm brown skin caught the light like it remembered joy even if she did not. I wanted to throw myself at her and tear the world apart. Instead, I let my pulse hammer in silence, watching.

She stood there, and slowly her body morphed, back was straighter. Her chest rose as she took in a deep breath. She met our eyes effortlessly. The fire dancing in them washed out her sadness.

"How do we get them back?" she asked, her voice low and cold.

It was almost devoid of emotion. Now knowing who her sister was, I wasn't surprised by the fire she had shown the night in the basement when she was seconds from tearing that sick fuck of a doctor apart.

The Kincaid family was what the people of the Sivad called "the mind". They were a bunch of cold, emotionless motherfuckers who could one moment show you care and kindness, and the next? Let's just say I was a tough son of a bitch, and even I knew I wouldn't survive one of their sessions.

Carter stood from the bed first, but I continued to lay there watching her, enjoying watching my little wolf turning into this version of herself.

"We?" he asked her.

Her eyes lowered into slits, and I held in a laugh because Carter was about to fuck around and find out. He must not have been watching her the same way that I was.

She tucked her luscious lips between her teeth, rubbing them together as her nose twitched.

"Did I stutter?" she asked, tilting her head.

Carter froze. That alone almost made me laugh out loud. He heard the shift in her voice and finally realized the woman in front of us was not the soft, trembling girl he liked to pretend she was four years ago.

"Did I?" she asked again.

"You did not, *yume-chan*," Carter acknowledged. He closed the distance between them using the knuckle of his index finger to lift her chin, so their eyes met. "We will get them back."

His promise spoke volumes. A promise I didn't need to cosign on because she knew we would do whatever was necessary to have our kids back.

Even if that meant burning down each country, one by one, until we found them.

Carter

"What do you fucking mean you can't fucking find anything!" G roared into Fin's face.

It had been two days... forty-eight hours since we both found out that we were fathers while simultaneously losing them.

Two days that our three year olds were missing at the hands of my so-called cousin.

Fin had been piecing what he grabbed from *Yume's* phone since G destroyed it before he could complete the duplication. I understood why G was pissed and the urgency of it all, but I knew like he should. Getting in Fin's face wasn't doing anything but asking to have yourself to become a literal digital ghost.

"G!" I said calmly, but was still firm.

"Listen here you fucking computer for brains. My kids are missing, my fucking kids! Find them, or we're gonna have some real problems, feel me!" he yelled, grabbing Fin by his staple graphic tee shirt.

Unphased, Fin pushed his glasses up and tilted his head to look at G. Glancing down to where his hands held his shirt and then back to his face, he quickly removed his hands. "Aye, I ken ye're losin' it, but grab me again, an' ye'll regret it, right?"

One thing I always observed was that Finlay was vastly underestimated. Even when I first met him, other than his skills with technology, I didn't understand why Henrik wanted him to be a part of the *Brorskap*. It wasn't until I saw that not only could he take anyone down hand to hand, but he was also a sharpshooter as well. Not to mention the wicked things he could do with internet connection.

G and him have had many times that they were seconds to coming to blows, and while I knew my brother was a killer, I also knew he shouldn't continue to underestimate Fin.

G stepped back nostrils flaring as he looked at Fin then back to his wall of monitors. G knew a lot about computers himself and could do light hacking, but the level we needed could only be done by Fin. If he was having a hard time, then I knew we were basically in the dark.

"What was the last known location?" I asked, still eerily calm.

"Judging by the fact he called from the sitter's phone, the lass's house," Fin answered, switching from his heavy Scottish brogue.

Kuso.

That feeling I had when I spoke on the phone earlier to the man who called himself my cousin came back. The anger was so tangible it was like I could hear the snake etched into my skin hissing.

I didn't like feeling out of control, and *this*. This situation put me in an unpredictable place.

Fin returned to his perusal, checking home cameras in *Yume's* neighborhood around the time of the call. I watched the screens move; some things I understood, some I didn't. I had no idea how Fin was able to follow everything because I was having a hard time trying to find anything in all the content on the screen.There were more codes than there was readable content littering the screen.

A part of me was fuming at *Yume*. The insatiable heat I felt a few days ago when I kissed her for the first time in four years, fought for dominance in my mind.

The feeling was irrational, especially since we left nothing for her to be able to track us. But knowing now that she was related to *the* Kincaid family let me know if she wanted to, she could have found us.

Keeping us in the dark left all three of them exposed. With being in the *Brorskap,* G and I had accumulated many enemies. If you add in my ties with the *Yakuza* and G's with the *Iron Saints,* who knows who the hell really took them?

"Yo, don't do that, man." I slightly turned to the sound of Banks' voice, eyes still trained on Fin's screens. "Ain't no way you could've known all this was gonna go down."

"*Shiru beki datta,*" I said lowly. The shame of failure tasted bitter on my tongue.

"How?" he questioned.

I chose not to answer him. Wasting time and energy with the pointless conversation did nothing for the situation at hand. The only answers I wanted to hear were from Fin.

An image came up on the screen, and my heart stopped. Two of the most beautiful little beings I had ever seen were smiling largely on the screen. Cake was on their faces and party hats on their heads. I couldn't see their faces clearly, but I could see how much the little boy reminded me of myself down to the hue of my hazel eyes and curly hair. The little girl had the same gray eyes of G, but her face was so much like Yume's.

Suddenly, the words said to me over the phone crashed into my mind. *Twins, of the same mother, but not father.* Lorelei already cleared any doubt I had when she confirmed the paternity with her sister.

Seeing their pictures solidified it and blew away any doubt I might have had. They were beautiful.

I looked to where G now stood, his attention transfixed on the image of the little humans we helped create.

"That was from their birthday this year. They're three." Both G and I whipped around at the sound of *Yume's* voice.

She stood in Fin's doorway. Her eyes were bloodshot–her skin flushed and red.

"*Lykáki,* you should be asleep." G moved swiftly to her.

"How can I sleep, Gerasimou?" she muttered. "How can I sleep not knowing if my babies are okay? If they are scared? If they're *hurt?*" She pushed the last word out like it pained her to even have to say it.

Her pain caused the room to feel smaller than it was. It had me ready to do whatever it took to never have her feel it again. As if she was a flame and I was a moth, I went to her. She looked up to me, and her eyes were weary, but also, there was a fire burning of readiness.

My hand cupped her cheek, and she leaned into it, attention flicking to G. Her trust evident in us shined bright.

"Aye, Carter!" Fin's voice pulled my attention back to the screen.

"*Hai*?" I asked.

"I got somethin'?"

We moved as one over to Fin's wall of monitors. I leaned in closer to one monitor that had a still shot of a beautiful two-story craftsman style home.

Lorelei's eyebrows furrowed as she also moved closer to the screen. "Is this a still of my house?"

"Aye," Fin answered in his normal light brogue. "I was able tae get into one of the camera systems of yer neighbour down the street."

He clicked a few keys, and a video started to play. It seemed like the video was taken from afar, but after a few more clicks, it was zoomed in and clear. We saw a young blonde enter her house, then Lorelei left her house shortly after.

Fin sped the feed up until the screen glitched for a second, then resumed.

A large black SUV pulled up in front of her house, parking. No hesitation. No circling the block. They knew exactly where they were going.

"There," I said.

Fin adjusted something, and the footage became smoother.

Four men stepped out. Their movements were uniform. Their heads turned in clean angles as they scanned the property. It was evident that these weren't amateurs; they were well trained.

Yume's eyes narrowed. I could feel the tension building in her body, but not panic. Calculation.

Fin reduced the speed again.

The four of them went to her door. Only one knocked as the others hid. After a moment, the blonde answered, spoke for a few seconds, and then she went to close the door, but he stopped it. When he tried to walk inside, the blonde tried to block the doorway. She yelled something over her shoulder, trying to push him. He grabbed her by the jaw and threw her back inside like she was nothing. The other men followed, their faces still not seen clearly.

Yume's breath hitched. Quiet. Sharp.

Two men came out after what felt like hours but was only minutes. That must have been the time when they called *Yume's* phone, each one carrying a bundled Wolfe and Dream. They were still and silent. Too silent. Too still.

They were being held like they were meaningless packages, not children. *Our* children! My vision darkened at the edges, but I stayed where I was. Rage now would help no one.

The third man came out with a limp Celeste draped over his shoulder. It was clear that they had drugged them with how little they moved. The men placed the twins inside the SUV first then followed with Celeste before they climbed in themselves.

"Where is the other guy?" *Yume* asked.

A few seconds passed before the man who knocked on the door came out. *Yume* gasped, and my eyes shot to her inquisitively. "I know him," she whispered.

"Who?" G demanded.

She cleared her throat. "Him." Fin froze the video on the mystery man's face. "I know him." She pointed at the screen.

"You know this mother fucker?" G gritted.

Lorelei rubbed her forehead, sighing deeply. "Yes, his name is—"

"Javier Giraldo, age thirty-two. Parents unknown. Lad is a member of the Giraldo Cartel." Fin cut her off. My brows furrowed at the familiarity of the name, but I couldn't place it.

"No, his name is Jason Crowne, and he is an anesthesiologist at Ithaca Grace Hospital," she corrected Fin. "I met him last year when I had to do an emergency neonatal surgery. There is no way that's the same person who took the twins. He doesn't even sound like the man who called me from Celeste's phone."

She was right; the man we spoke to had a deep Latin accent, but everyone but her in this room knew how easy it was to blend in when needed or wanted. But we all just watched the same footage of him and his goons taking them.

"I get it. It's actually simple to switch up accents." Fin spoke in the most American accent I'd heard him do to date. "Not to mention it seems he may have used an alias to get close to you."

Yume straightened her back with understanding. She continued to stare at the image of the fucker who wouldn't live to see Christmas. Now that we had a face and name, we were that much closer to getting the twins back.

"Is there more?" she asked Fin.

"Aye." Fin pressed play, and the video continued.

The man we now know as Javier, turned back to the entrance of the house, and without having to see the rest of the video, I knew exactly what he was going to do. Reaching in his pocket, he pulled out a small silver object. Turning slightly so we could see his face, he gave a slick smile. He flicked his finger on the wheel of the object in his hand, sparking a flame, then tossed it into the doorway.

Lorelei's breathing leveled, like the air had been sucked out of her lungs as she watched her home, the one she raised our children in, go up in flames. The light from the monitor reflected in her eyes illuminating the pain she felt.

"Are you able to track that vehicle?" she asked, voice thick with emotion.

"Workin' on it," Fin replied. "I need a minute."

G leaned against the desk, to her right, arms crossed, watching her with fond curiosity.

I stepped closer, not touching her, unable to help but be close to her.

"We are going to get them back, right?" she asked, her voice shaky.

She turned to face me, waiting for my answer. I nodded my head sharply. G came closer, fitting in our puzzle perfectly. We stood there staring at the woman we were perfectly obsessed with, making a silent vow to her, to *us*... that we would get our children back, while also wishing we could fix it now.

For the first time since the twins were taken, *Yume* smiled. It wasn't one that fully reached her eyes and made them shine brightly. It was shaky at best, but it was enough that it said she trusted in us to fulfill our promise.

Lorelei

Four years later, and I still couldn't stand to hear *All I want for Christmas* play during the holiday season. Not to mention on every single social channel since November first, all you heard was content creators using the audio where she screamed '*it's timmmmeeeeee*'.

I was sitting in the vast kitchen at the island of the Davis manor being forced to eat as the sound played quietly from somewhere I couldn't pinpoint. Carter and G deposited me here with stern faces and hard eyes letting me know I had no choice but to sit my ass here and eat whatever Hans made.

"Oooo... Hansieeee, what you making?" I smiled at the voice.

A small whirlwind of chaotic energy and wild red curls came barreling into the kitchen taking a seat next to me on the high back stools lined against the counter. Not even seconds from her entering the space, the large blonde she called *Big* came behind her.

Saysha Devereaux was as fiery as her hair manifested. I remember the hell she would cause when she was younger with her 'take no shit' attitude that was bigger than life. She was just a breath of fresh air.

Hans smiled brightly at her. "Saysha, hallo. I am making eggs, bacon, ham, French toast, and a few other things. It's almost done."

"Good, I'm starving!" she exclaimed.

Hans went back to what he was doing, and Saysha turned in her seat to face me. I didn't turn to meet her gaze because I knew what I would find if I did... pity.

Every time I was forced to leave the room I had taken up residence in, I was met with pity glances from the staff in the house. The only time I felt remotely okay was when I checked in on Faven and her girls. The boys were reluctant to let me check on them because they didn't think mentally I could. They weren't wrong because I bawled like a baby the moment I got back to the room after, but I had a duty to give Faven the best care. Not only because she was the leader of the Sivad Syndicate but because as a Black woman, we never received the care we deserved in the medical world.

Either way, it killed me to see her hold her twins when I couldn't hold mine. We were on day four of the twins being gone and still hadn't gotten any closer to finding them.

I felt like I couldn't fucking breathe. Like I didn't have the right to when I didn't know if they were. *Fuck*! I didn't even want to think that was a possibility. They were okay; G and Carter told me they would get them back to us.

"So, how long you just gon' sit here sulking?"

My head snapped to where the question came from. Saysha was sitting there staring as she chomped down on a piece of thick cut bacon. She had a bored expression on her face like she was annoyed by me or something.

Instantly, my skin pricked, and my ears heated. How fucking dare she ask me some shit like that so callously.

"Excuse me?" I had to ask her because maybe I heard it wrong.

"Guhl, please, you ain't deaf," she said, rolling her eyes.

"Saysha, I am not in the mood to do this with you right now," I stated, turning back in my seat to find a plate of food had been set in front of me.

She scoffed. "Your ass don't seem to be in the mood to do a damn thing if you ask me."

Choosing to ignore her, I picked up my fork, scooping eggs up, and put them in my mouth. They were good, perfectly cooked and fluffy, but how I felt, I might as well had been eating cardboard.

"You see this shit, Big?" Saysha asked her blonde shadow.

He didn't say anything, he just huffed his agreement.

I took a deep breath and sipped the freshly squeezed orange juice Hans gave me.

"I mean, shit, it makes sense though if you could hide ya kids from their father, then clearly you don't give a fuck if they missing. Hell, maybe she—"

The slam of my palm to the marble countertop cut her off. I was livid.

"I don't know what the fuck your problem is, Saysha," I spoke low and menacingly. "But you have one more time to open your mouth about my kids, and I'ma know something."

"My problem is *you*."

I stood from my seat, and she stood from hers. Her face still held a look of annoyance as she looked me up and down.

We were only a few inches difference in height, me being a few inches taller than her. However, the way she sized me up, it was like we were eye to eye.

Disrespecting Faven's home wasn't on my docket today, and I was all for letting Saysha have it, but the moment she spewed that fowl shit out her mouth about me as a mother, all bets were off. I was on go and ready for whatever.

"You want to repeat that shit?" I gritted.

Big stood up. "Red." I swear that was the first time I heard him speak.

Without taking her eyes off of me, she responded to him, "I'm good, Ivor."

"You might want to listen to your guard dog, because the way I'm feeling right now...."

"What you gonna do, huh?" she taunted me. "I'll tell you. You gon' go back to that room and sulk. Then ya gonna cry to thing one and two and have them come press me about ya bullshit."

I advanced on her, my anger rising. Pointing my finger in her face let off how I felt. "Fuck you, Saysha. How dare you chastise me about what the fuck I am going through? My fucking kids are gone. I don't know where the fuck they are, and it's probably my fault they were taken. So, you are damn fucking right I am going to sulk, because what the fuck else can I do?!"

By the time I got to the end of my rant, spit was flying out of my mouth on her. My voice was elevated, but I wasn't exactly yelling. None of it affected her. If anything, she looked more bored by it.

"Boo fucking hoo. Hans, you got one of them dish cloths back there?" She held her hand out, and this man really gave her one. "Here, take this and wipe ya fucking tears 'cause I for sure ain't."

My eyes glared at the blue cloth she held out to me. I slapped it from her hands. "I don't need you to do a damn thing for me other than getting the fuck out my face." I pushed her, but she barely moved.

Laughing, she dusted the shoulder of the sweater she wore off. "Shit, maybe ya weak ass should do nothing but sulk 'cause how you gonna fight for ya babies like that, eh?"

"Or maybe, this weak ass should beat the fuck out you for coming at me like that?"

"Don't talk about it, bitch, run ya hands."

I lunged for her but was lifted from the ground by strong arms.

"*Lykáki,*" Gerasimou spoke sternly in my ear. "Calm down."

"Let me go, Gerasimou. This bitch came in here fucking with me like I won't wipe the floor with her ass."

Saysha laughed again. "Beat me? Bitch, you couldn't even push me. No wonder ya in the shit you in now. Weak ass bitches make my ass itch."

"I got your bitch." I fought to get free from Gerasimou's hold, to no avail. "Let me the fuck go!" I screamed into the air.

Punching and clawing at him, I attempted to free myself so I could get at this bitch. Every ounce of despair and anger I had been feeling the last four days, no fuck that... the last four years I was about to unleash on her.

"Let her go, G," Saysha said. "If this is what she wants, then so be it."

G went to let me go, but I froze when I saw Henrik step into the kitchen. "How is it possible I can hear you all clearly from my office?" he asked all of us.

"It ain't shit, mini giant. I was just seconds from showing this weakling what it was," Saysha taunted me further.

I went to lunge at her, but Gerasimou caught me, pulling me into his chest.

"Look, I'm not even going to begin to give a fuck what you all have going on, but I know if you break anything in this kitchen, it'll upset my wife, and then you'll have to deal with me. Take that shit to the sparring room."

I didn't know where the sparring room was, but I knew that once I got there, I was gonna beat this bitch's ass.

Lorelei

"Damn, she beatin' shorty's ass!" Someone exclaimed when my back hit the mat for the millionth time.

I quickly leaped from the soft mat, that felt anything but soft every time Saysha landed me on my ass. A smirk played on her face as she looked cool, calm, and collected. There was barely a curl out of place in the pineapple she had put her hair in when we got down here.

"Damn, guhl, I was for sure you was gonna show my ass something. But I guess I had it right that you weak as hell," she taunted.

Wiping the sweat that accumulated on my forehead, I lowered my eyes into slits. Yeah, she had been putting me on my ass since we came down here, but I didn't give a fuck.

"Fuck you!" I spat.

"No thanks, *Cher*, you don't have big enough balls to ride this ride." She winked.

It enraged me that she thought this shit was a joke. My eye twitched as the anger fueled me. Saysha got into a fighting stance, and I followed suit. I was done playing with her ass. I advanced on her, throwing a punch she dodged easily.

We went on like that for a while, me throwing hits and Saysha dodging them and saying some smart shit to get under my skin.

When she went to sweep kick me, I jumped back, and when she stood, I back handed the shit out of her.

Slowly, she turned to face me, a trickle of blood dripped from the corner of her lip. She used her thumb to dab at it and looked at it like she was measuring the pain, testing it.

"Oh. So the kitty does have claws. Well, don't hold back now, Cher. Let me know something."

And I did. In doing so, Saysha let me know she'd been holding back this entire time. But I didn't hold back either, matching her as best as I could, even though I knew I wasn't on her level. I hadn't been keeping up with my training.

When I started to slow, Saysha barked, "Don't give up, beat my fucking ass. I don't care how tired you are," snapping me back.

Somehow, that fueled me.

"You think your babies care that you're tired and hurt? Do you think they give a fuck that you're sulking? Do you think they care about anything other than you finding them and keeping them safe?"

Her words hit me differently this time. She wasn't just fucking with me to be a bitch. She was forcing me to get out the grief I was feeling. And even every tear I'd dropped was warranted, but what the fuck was that doing for my kids?

My exhaustion was nothing compared to what they were going through out there. And if I continued down this path I had been, it wouldn't just be me paying the price.

I clenched my fists tightly, allowing her words to sink in. The fire building inside of me turned into the very thing I would be using to help me get them back. Pain was temporary. Fear was temporary. Losing my babies was temporary.

No more was I looking to Carter and G to solve this while I sat in my tears. Time to show Javier what finding out was about when you fucked around. I was a mother on a rampage, and I would burn this whole fucking world down to get them back.

Saysha pulled me in a hug tightly. As much as I wanted to cry, I held my tears in. There would be a time for that, but not until they were ones of joy from having my kids back in my arms.

"Thank you," I whispered in her ear.

She pulled out of our embrace holding me at arm's length. "No thank you necessary. Just don't ever let me catch you slacking again. We are going to get them babies back. No one takes a child of the Sivad and not feel that shit through their entire blood line, old and new."

She wiped the tear I hadn't noticed escaped before she walked away. G and Carter attempted to approach me ready to take me in their arms, but I held my hand out stopping them. My eyes darted around the sparring room until it landed on the door to leave. I noticed the few on-lookers were now gone, besides us three.

I needed a moment to breathe and to figure out how to settle the rage that was brewing in me. The sadness was still there, the grief feeling as if it had a grip on my lungs it wouldn't ever let go of until my babies were back.

The rage, however, coiled through my entire being, and I didn't have room for any emotion other than keeping the burning flame I felt alive. I saw the love and obsession shining in their eyes as if we hadn't missed a step in each other's lives. I could feel the entanglement of our souls, tethered indefinitely together.

It would only take one touch from either of them, and I would succumb to it and would be no use to our children.

Plus, there was so much trauma between us that none of us had time to break down and heal from.

"Please..." I choked out. "I need a moment."

Turning, I ambled towards the exit. My hand barely brushed the handle before I felt myself being pushed, roughly but not to the point of hurt, against the cold steel of the door.

"The only moment you need is the one we allow you, *Lykáki*," Gerasimou whispered in my ear. His breath ghosting my ear caused goosebumps to raise.

"Oh, *Yume*, our time gone seemed to give you false assurance that you ever had a choice. For now, we will give you the time you requested, based on the more pressing matters we face." Carter was in my other ear, and my body went haywire in only the way having them both this close to me could cause.

"And, I, for one, cannot wait to remind you that you are ours now and forever."

They both kissed the crook of my neck and left. I stayed pinned against the door afraid to see if they truly left through an unknown door or if they were waiting to devour me.

Either way, I left myself once I recollected myself, pushing the feeling they brought to the recesses of my mind and tapped into that rage again.

Determined, I went to check on the progress of finding my kids, hoping any development had been made.

G

I fought every inch of my instincts as I watched Lykáki leave and not pin her against the wall to fuck the hurt evident in her. The pain in her voice when she yelled at Saysha and when she told us she needed a moment triggered a savior complex I never felt with anyone but her.

Witnessing the turmoil she'd been in the last few days—and not being able to fix it instantly—had me ready to ride out and fuck some shit up. Her silent cries, the way she stared off blankly, stripped of the vibrant woman we fell for, felt like knives carving through my chest. Hell... at this point, I'd have preferred to use sex to rid us all from feeling the loss instead of this emptiness I knew we all felt in the absence of our twins.

Fuck, I had twins. I would never be able to not be in awe of that shit. Me being a father wasn't anything I would have ever foreseen, not after how I grew up. The sick shit people were capable of. And even if only one of them were biologically mine, both Carter and I felt the same that they belonged to both of us just like their *μαμά*.

They belonged to us, and we dropped the ball. No matter how you sliced it, we'd failed Lorelei. We'd failed our kids.

"We fucked up, man," I muttered. Didn't need to say his name—Carter knew who I meant.

"*Sí*, brother... we have," he said, voice low, threaded with guilt. He only slipped into Spanish when he was in his feelings, and right now, he was a hurricane inside, holding it just enough. He stared at the door she'd walked through like he could pull her back by sheer will.

"We shouldn't have left her," I admitted.

Carter turned his head slightly toward me. "Hmm." That being all he said before returning his gaze to the door.

That *hmm* to anyone else would have appeared like he was agreeing, but I knew better... that slight inflection. Something was off. I knew Carter. I knew his moves, his tone, his thoughts before he even spoke.

"What is it, Javone?" His jaw twitched at my use of his first name.

"Giraldo." He turned to me. "The Giraldo Cartel. *Esta es la familia de mi madre.*"

"Okay, they're your mother's family. And what does that shit have to do with you?"

"Do you not get it, Dimitri?" he snapped. "My blood knew. Knew they belong to me and took them to fucking sell them!"

"Okay, and their blood will spill for that shit. It happened, so what are we going to do to fix it?" When he didn't answer right away, I continued. "I'll tell you what. We're gonna find that mother fucker, get our kids back and light up anyone who tries to interfere, feel me?"

Carter studied me for a tick but nodded his agreement. I saw the battle he was facing in his eyes, I felt it myself.

Something in the pit of my stomach told me this shit was bigger than what we thought.

My phone vibrated in my jeans pocket, and when I checked it, Fin had texted Carter and me.

Fin

I've got something.

There wasn't a need to answer; he knew we were coming.

"Look, we can sit and get our panties in a bunch that ya blood is coming for us, but we know what the fuck to do. Same thing we always do."

I held his stare until he confirmed. "Clean our plate."

"You damn right!" I clapped him on the shoulder before exiting the sparring room to Fin's room.

"Aye, fellas, I got something," Fin said the moment we stepped into his office, without turning around.

We took either side of him, arms folded, waiting to see if he had anything worth our time.

"What you got?"

"Did you find something?" Carter and I asked at the same time.

"Sorta. This was sent to me about twenty minutes ago."

"Show us," Carter demanded.

He clicked a few keys, and a website came up on his main screen. The only thing on it was a large flip clock that took up majority of the screen, counting down the time with every flip of a number. Nothing else.

"What are we looking at?" I asked.

"This site from the darkest part of the web I had trouble even getting into," he explained. "Only for it to be a countdown."

Carter turned to me, and we silently communicated. If Fin had trouble getting into anything concerning the digital world, then that meant he had indeed found something. It was if that something was about our twins or something else.

"What's the countdown for?" Carter asked.

"Per my resource," Fin started.

"Who is your resource?" I asked. While I was pleased we might have something to go off of, I didn't like not knowing who the fuck had their nose in our business.

"I can't tell you that, lad," Fin responded. "Know I've vetted them myself though, so no worries. They sent me this site after they heard through the *Blackwire* there was a sale of the rarest and most unique merchandise on the market. Now, we don't know exactly what is being sold, but based on the fact the twins are technically a rare phenomenon, I think it may be a lead. Once the clock stops, the information for the merchandise will be revealed, and bids will start."

I scratched at the overgrown scruff on my jaw, in desperate need of a shave, blinking at every second that flipped on the timer. If you were in the criminal underworld, you knew what the *Blackwire* was.

The *Blackwire* was an intricate word to mouth system controlled by the *Keepers*. If you had anything you needed to sell, buy, or wanted a meeting, you would go through The *Keepers*, and they would relay it to whoever was appropriate. They also had a hand in setting up these auctions in the hotels they owned because of the neutrality of the space.

"Location?" Carter asked.

"The auction is virtual, but I believe it's at one of the—"

"Citadel hotels?"

A red hue crept up Fin's neck. "Aye." He confirmed with a sharp nod.

"Confirm if it is indeed one of the Citadels, and let us know," Carter said before leaving.

I knew for sure he was going to go tell Lorelei the new development, and while I normally would be right behind him, I needed to check Fin's head.

"You sure you can trust this person?" I probed.

He didn't answer right away, the clicking of his computer keys the only sound to be heard.

A smirk formed at the corner of my lips because I knew exactly who his source was. He was fucking crazy to pursue her after what happened to her the last time she got mixed up with us.

"Well, I'ma let your nerdy ass get to it then. Oh, before I forget." His fingers paused, waiting for me to continue. "Let Ayela know if anything happens to my kids, I'll make that ass kicking Faven and Saysha gave her look like child's play."

He stuck up his middle finger, and it was all the confirmation I needed. If he wanted to latch on to that posh ass girl, that was his business. And while there wasn't much off the table for me when it came to a job, I drew the line at women. We had female assassins who took care of that.

But for my kids... for *Lykáki*, I'd wipe the entire Nash bloodline out.

Carter

Where the hell is she? I left the sitting room after checking the bedroom, and *Yume* wasn't in either. She told us she needed space, and I hoped like hell it didn't mean leaving the Davis manor.

We knew who took the twins and it would be suicide got them to come within ten miles of the Davis property line. Knowing that information did nothing to ease the thudding in my heart as I went to the kitchen to see if I saw her there.

Nothing.

"Carter."

I stiffened before turning around. Deidre Davis stood there with a pleasant smile on her face. I bowed out of respect, but she was the last person I wanted to see.

Where you'd find the eldest of the Davis sisters, you would find Cyrus Monro, and even on a good day, I lacked the patience to deal with his maniacal behavior.

"Deidre."

"You do not have to bow at me, Carter. I'm not Faven," she joked.

She was correct; I didn't need to bow to her as I would the leader of the Sivad. However, she still warranted respect, and if my father hadn't taught me anything, it was that respect was always a priority.

Meaning, whether I *had* to or not wasn't her call.

"Is there something I can help you with?"

"Walk with me?" She turned and walked towards the east wing where all the offices were located. While she framed it as a question, it was anything but, and I knew to follow her.

We moved down the hall in silence. She didn't explain, and I didn't ask. I kept glancing down intersecting corridors, hoping to catch sight of Lorelei's loc's, her walk, anything.

When we came to one of the office doors, Deidre used her thumb print to open it. She held it long enough for me to enter, then closed it behind us. The lock clicked softly in the silence.

This was my first time in Deidre's office. After the explosion, Faven and Henrik decided to turn this entire wing, with some spaces added, into offices.

"Have a seat, Carter." Deidre moved towards a small seating area set up in front of a low-burning fireplace. Two deep chairs faced the flames, upholstered in one of those bold, artsy patterns she liked—striking but somehow still refined. A sculptural black side table sat between them, catching the firelight in sharp angles. That was where an envelope waited, placed deliberately in the center as if it were part of the décor.

Following her, I sat in the chair across from hers.

"I don't want to take up too much of your time." She leaned forward reaching for a white envelope.

She extended her hand, the envelope resting lightly in her palm. "This came for you."

I glanced down at it, then back at her, raising an eyebrow. My silent question hung between us: *What is this?*

She met my stare without flinching, one brow arched.

This wasn't the elegant, reserved Deidre the world expected. Maybe she had been once—but whatever memory had returned three years ago had sharpened her into someone just as cunning as her husband.

I didn't trust her... not entirely. My father used to run training sessions that taught me to recognize danger before it spoke. And right now... something about this envelope screamed danger.

Whether that danger was from her or something else entirely was up for question.

Letting out an exaggerated huff, she told me where the envelope came from. "Your father had this sent to me via private courier. There were strict instructions to give this to you privately." Gone was her playful mirth, replacing energy only a Davis woman could possess.

Taking the envelope from her, I turned it over to find it sealed by my father's personal sealant. Opening it, I read the contents, and I was more confused than when she first presented it to me.

The contents were written in my father's handwriting. He chose to use *Jōdai Nihongo,* a historical Japanese language from the ancient *Kojiki* and *Man'yōshū* texts.

Takahashi-chan,

By the time this reaches you, I trust you will have already exhausted every traditional route available to you. That is good. A man should act before he reaches for ghosts.

There is only one person who can give you the answers you seek.

You will not want this. Your pride has always been your most stubborn companion. But necessity does not concern itself with pride, and neither does blood.

Contained below is a number.

Call it.

She will answer.

I will not explain further in writing. You know as well as I do that ink is a liability. What I will say is this: the woman on the other end of that line has waited thirty-four years for the chance to hear your voice. She is... not without fault. Neither am I. But she is capable of helping you in ways that neither you nor your brothers-in-arms can imagine.

Do not let old wounds keep you from protecting what is yours.

Claro Giraldo : +57 320 674 1958

— Otōsan

I read the letter once, twice... then three times before folding it and placing it carefully back into the envelope it came in.

Words evaded me as I stared at the fire burning in the hearth. The flames flickered like it had its own heartbeat putting me in a trance as my mind went into a spiral over the letter itself as well and the contents.

Deidre didn't attempt to fill the silence with meaningless chatter, and I was thankful for it. Too many things filtered through my mind, and I didn't hold the capacity to talk to her just yet.

"Why was it sent to you?" I finally asked her.

Removing my attention from the fire to her, I was met with a warm smile. "Partly because I am standing in place while Faven is on maternity leave. But mainly because your father knows and trusts my discretion."

Pulling my lips into my mouth, I nodded. I rubbed my chest without thinking, the old ache returning, one I had not felt this sharply since I was a boy.

Deidre stood from her seat, placing her hand on my shoulder giving it a gentle squeeze. Her expression told me she understood how I was feeling, and I was sure after skeletons that poured from her own family closets, she did.

"Javone." I looked up to her. "I won't begin to understand what you're feeling, but I also know of your upbringing. As I stated, I do know your father. My mother had plenty of meetings with him I was in attendance for. I also know your mother, Claro.

"Hear her out. Our parents, no matter how powerful they are, are just people who have made mistakes or had to make hard choices that seemed impossible. I'll give you the room. Other than Cyrus, no one can enter this room but me."

With that, she left me. The door clicked shut behind her.

Silence pressed into the room. Heavy. Suffocating.

I stared at the envelope in my hand. Its contents replayed in my mind on a loop.

My mother.

A stranger.

A ghost.

And apparently, the one person who had answers about my children's disappearance. I exhaled slowly, forcing my thumb to hit the call button before I could second-guess myself.

The line rang once.

Twice.

Three times.

Then—

A soft inhale. A voice like warm honey weighted by a thick Latin accent came through.

"...*Takahashi-chan*?"

My grip tightened around the phone until my knuckles burned.

"Do not call me that." My voice came out low, clipped, controlled.

A shaky, relieved breath answered me.

"Then tell me what I may call you, *hijo*."

My stomach dropped.

Son.

I hated that one word hit something inside me.

I hated that she said it like she'd been holding it in for decades.

"I'm not calling for a reunion," I bit out. "You told my father you had information."

"I do," she said softly. "Your father told me what happened."

A long silence stretched between us. You could feel the many words we both needed to say, but neither of us did.

Then she added, her voice thick with unshed tears, "I have waited thirty years to hear your voice again, *hijo*. To apologize for the choices your father and I made. And while I know this call isn't for that, please allow me to show you by assisting in finding your children. For you... I will tell you everything."

Claro Giraldo

A lone tear streamed down my face the moment my *hijo's* voice came through the line. Thirty years it had passed since I last talked to him, since the last time I heard his little voice say in the cutest way '*te quiero, Mama, te quiero*'. Based upon the coldness of his tone when he snapped at me, I was sure he didn't remember that. Even though I hadn't been in his life the last thirty years, I very much was until he was four.

I stayed with him as long as I possibly could before it became too suspicious and I was made to fulfil my duty as the heir to the Giraldo Cartel. Not a single day went by that I didn't think about him. How was he doing? If he missed me. The way his beautiful hazel eyes mirrored my own. For the first four years of his life, I went back and forth from Cartagena to Yokohama whenever I could to see him.

However, in this world, we all had a part to play, and mine was mapped out for me by my father before I was even born.

I closed my eyes, forcing myself to gain control of my emotions. It was something I had been doing for years. I knew once I gave Tahashi the okay to give our son my number, it wasn't going to be met with open arms.

In his eyes, I abandoned him, although my reasonings were to protect him, and I had sent my aunt on my mother's side to help raise him. The damage of me not only leaving but staying away was done.

His silence was so profound, I had to look to ensure he hadn't hung up. After a beat, he spoke again. "*Tuviste algo que ver con que se llevaran a mis hijos*?"

My heart stopped hearing him speak Spanish so fluently. I didn't doubt that Paola would teach him to be fluent but actually hearing how well he could, filled me with pride and gave me hope that he held a part of me in his heart.

That feeling quickly ended when he repeated his question. To be honest, I was extremely offended that he would think I would have a hand in harming anything that came from him. From me. From his father.

"Javone," I said sharply. "You think I would have anything to do with causing harm to *mis nietos*? How dare you insinuate—"

"I don't know shit about you, *Claro,*" he spat.

"I am your mother!"

"You are the lady who threw me away the moment I came crawling out your despicable pussy."

"That is not true."

"I do not care what is fucking true and what is not!" he yelled. "What I want to know is where my fucking children are, and I swear, *Madre,* if one hair on their heads are harmed, I will fillet each layer of your skin and fucking feed it to you, *puta*. Now cut the fucking endearment and talk."

I had to hand it to him. The way he was so callous and cold, threatening me without a care for the repercussions anyone else would have faced talking to me in this manner, showed me that he was very much a product of me and Tahashi.

"Very well, *hijo*. I will give you the information I have." I complied, but only enough to show him that I understood how high emotions were. But again, I was the *Jefa* of the Giraldo Cartel and had killed a motherfucker for looking at me too long. Son or no son, he would show respect. "*Pero*, make no mistake that this will be the last time you ever flick your tongue to speak to me in such a manner. Do you understand?"

He switched to Japanese, cursing me, and again, I understood his grievances, but I would not bend on this. "*Me entiendes, carajo*?"

"As long as you tell me what I need to know," he stated flatly.

I was happy we were on the phone rather than in person. Being on the phone, I was able to mask the fact that I was quite pleased that he didn't cower to me.

"I know who took your children," I told him.

"You aren't telling me anything I don't already know, Claro. My so-called cousin took them as revenge that we stopped his latest trafficking scheme."

"*Primo*?" I asked, confused.

"Yes. So whoever one of your relatives he belongs to will need to start funeral preparations. Because the moment my children are safe, I will end their miserable lives."

I knew the outcome of what would happen when they would come for their children. I made peace with it. Even if that meant losing a part of me in the process.

I also knew that I needed to clear up a few things because I knew that Javier would indeed spin this in a way that was beneficial to him.

"So, you know it was Javier who took them?" I asked.

"And you know where he took them."

He didn't ask, he stated. And while I was the head of the Cartel, it came at a price to be.

Javier and his father were my price.

"I do not know the exact location, but I can get him to bring them back."

A chuckle left him. It wasn't one of joy or even mirth, but dark. It was so dark that it made the hairs on my arms stand. I wasn't scared, not much scared me anymore. But like any smart person, you know when someone had the ability to strike fear and land.

"You say you don't know where my children are, Claro, and at this point, you have wasted the time I could have used to help find them. With every second that this conversation goes by, the little bit of fucks I had to care if you continued breathing or not diminishes. Give me something useful, or I'll come to that nice little hidden room behind the false bookcase in Cartagena, the one you think no one knows about. I'll open it, Claro... and you won't have time to run."

"You do not scare me, Javone."

"I do not give one single fuck if I am scaring you, Claro. I mean what I say. How will you get Javier to bring my children to you? Because either you aren't as in control of your men as you think, or you helped that son of a bitch and you want me to spare your life."

He wasn't wrong in one aspect. I wasn't in control of my men. Not all, but enough that this shit happened.

"Javier... is." I stopped and hesitated. I wasn't sure I wanted to tell him the truth, not because I cared what happened to Javier, but because I didn't want the reaction I knew would come once Javone heard it.

"Tick-tock, Claro."

I took a deep breath and prayed for forgiveness. "I can make Javier come to me with the children because I am his mother, Javone."

The phone went silent again, but this time, I could feel the anger pulsing from the other end.

"He is my what? " he finally asked.

"Your *hermano*. Javier is your hermano, Javone." My heart rate accelerated.

I heard what sounded like crashing in the background, mixed with a range of cursing in both Spanish and Japanese.

Gnawing on my lip, I continued to wait as I heard my son, my oldest child, cause wreckage wherever he was. I didn't utter a single word; I just allowed him to get out how he was feeling.

I knew him learning he had siblings, yes... *siblings* because he had two sisters as well, would anger him. Who wouldn't be angry to learn that the mother who essentially abandoned them as a child went on to have three more after you? To not only have them but to be present in their lives.

Javone deserved an explanation. He deserved to hear it from me that it wasn't because I loved him. Hell it wasn't because I loved my *esposo*. Actually. I despised Hector. But that story wasn't for now. It wasn't about me but about the feud Javier one-sidedly had with his brother.

After a few moments, I could hear his heavy breathing come through the phone. There was a rustling sound of him picking it up, then he called my name. His breathing was abruptly even, his tone cold.

"Claro," he said.

"*Si*, Javone."

"You have forty-eight hours to get my children into your line of sight. By the forty-ninth, you will be one less child. And if I find out you had a single fucking hand in my children leaving the protective arms of their mother's, I will shred ever single ounce of that fucking organization into nothing, and when you have nothing but the tattered clothes on your back, I will slit you throat, *slowly* while you watch G slaughter each member of your family before I finish you off with a smile on my fucking face."

I swallowed hard. For the first time in many years, I was scared. Not for my life. I didn't have anything to do with Javier's sick scheme. But for my daughters, my mother, my *familia*. Because I had a sneaky suspicion that Javone didn't care if I was guilty or not. I had already committed a horrendous crime in his eyes, and I was sure he would make me pay with their blood for it.

"I will reach out to you exactly when and where as soon as I know." I spoke clearly despite the lump in my throat.

He didn't say anything. He ended the call, and that's when I allowed my emotions to get the best of me.

"*Taiyo-chan*."The softness of his voice wrapped around me.

"He hates me," I whispered, hugging myself tightly.

As always, I didn't even know he was here, but that was so much like Tahashi. He always showed up unexpectedly. Always appeared just when I needed him. I wasn't surprised at all that he came since this place was gifted to me by him. It was a place I went when I needed to breathe and not be the head of a ruthless criminal organization.

Pulling me into his arms, I didn't fight him. The embrace gave me a peace I hadn't known in a while, not since the last time I saw him.

He kissed the top of my wild coils before lifting my head until I met his dark brown orbs.

"He may feel that way now, *Taiyo-Chan*. Once he learns of why we had to do things this way, he will feel differently." I heard his words, and as much as I wanted to believe them... I knew differently.

Javone would never forgive me or Tahasi, especially when he learned the entire story.

"*Mamá*!" The call of my name caused me to pull away from Tahashi.

My fifteen-year-old twin daughters, Julieta and Jessenia, came barreling in the room. They stopped abruptly when they noticed Tahashi.

They could only see his back, but it was all they needed to know exactly who he was.

"*Otōchan*!" they squealed, jumping on Tahashi.

They missed him as much as I knew he missed them. And this was what I was afraid to tell Javone more than anything. This was the deepest betrayal.

"*Mis hijas*!" he replied to his daughters in perfect Spanish, giving them love.

Lorelei

"One hot chocolate with crème brûlée cream." Saysha handed me the double cup filled with the hot sweet goodness.

"Thank you so much." I took the cute gingerbread man mug.

I blew on the delicious smelling concoction and sipped it. The hot chocolate was perfectly warm and did something to my broken soul as I swallowed it.

Needing more of that feeling and not caring about savoring it, I took large gulps until my mug was empty.

"Well, shit... you really did need to get out," Saysha joked.

After my encounter with Carter and Gerasimou, I went to my room, showered, and dressed. When I couldn't take being in the silence anymore, I left to find something to do and found Saysha on her way out.

She invited me to go with her and Ivor to the Commons to a bakery. Needing to get out of that house, I jumped at the chance. I knew that Carter and G were most likely going crazy looking for me, but I just needed a minute to fucking breathe.

I needed them to not look at me with the guilt they felt. To not see our babies eyes every time I looked at them. To not have to war with feelings that should no longer be so damn prevalent.

"So, have you been a midwife long?" Saysha asked.

Her question caught me off guard. "Uh..."

"Damn, I hope you don't freeze like that during birth." She threw her head back and cackled.

Her ginger curls bounced around her head with not a care in the world if she drew attention to herself.

Based on the current state of my life, I should be worried that she had patrons of the bakery all looking at us. But I didn't. Saysha proved to me not even a few hours ago that though she seemed girly and was petite, she was a force to be reckoned with.

"No," I chortled. "I don't. I've been a midwife for almost a year in February, but before that, I was one of the top neonatal surgeons in the country."

"Ooo, so a beautiful Black woman who is smart and can fight, I like." Saysha held her hand up for me to high five, and I returned the gesture.

"Thank you! I love what I do," I beamed.

We continued to talk while Ivor sat there silently with us. He was surveying the area but also vigilantly watching Saysha's every move.

They seemed so much like an odd fitting couple. He was burly and ruggedly handsome with a serious demeanor, while she was cute, small, and loud. But at the same time, they worked so well together. It kind of reminded me of me and the boys.

After we finished our drinks, Saysha declared we should walk around the commons and sightsee. She wanted to check out the tree even though it was still too early in the day for the lights to be on, and see the Christmas decorations put up.

Ivor looked anything but pleased and had no problem voicing it. "Red." Just that one word said all it needed to, and Saysha ignored it like he hadn't spoken at all.

Grabbing my hand, she practically dragged me out of the bakery.

Making our rounds, we looked at every Christmas decoration displayed in the commons before coming up to the reasonably sized ice-skating rink. I didn't know how, but I was having a good time.

Did I feel a tinge of guilt? Yes.

But I needed to clear my head, and this was helping.

The sky was starting to turn that golden hue, and we decided it was time to return to the Davis manor. I made a mental reminder to bring the twins back here when they came home.

Since we moved here in February of this year, we missed seeing the Commons during the holiday season. Not that they would have really appreciated it since they were only two, but now that they were a bit bigger, they were starting to love the aspect of Christmas, and I knew they would love it.

As we pulled up to the entrance of the manor, Carter and Gerasimou were standing on the steps, deep frowns on their handsome faces.

"Looks like someone's in trouble," Saysha teased.

I couldn't even say anything because the looks they were giving me through the heavy tint of the back window had me squeezing my thighs together.

Before Ivor could park fully, they were there opening my door and pulled me quickly from the car. Gerasimou picked me up, throwing me over his shoulder without a single word, and Carter slapped my ass so hard the reverberation echoed through the cool winter air.

"Don't do my girl too bad, Things One and Two!" Saysha yelled to their back. I could see her, and just before the door shut, I saw Ivor lift her off the ground and throw her over his shoulder as well.

"Gerasimou, put me down!" I demanded.

Carter slapped my ass again coupled with a glare that told me talking wasn't optional and gave no room for demands on my part.

Being the smart woman I was, I closed my mouth after I yelped from the sharp slap.

Gerasimou dropped me onto the bed hard enough that the mattress bounced, the shock rolling up my spine. I scrambled, trying to regain my balance, but before I could fully sit up, Carter was on me.

His hands slammed into the mattress on either side of my hips. One near my thigh, one by my shoulder, caging me in. He leaned in, his nose to mine, and I had no choice but to allow the closeness.

"Do not leave this fucking house again and not tell us," he gritted.

My heart slammed rapidly against my chest not from fear but because I was turned on. This was the first time I heard Carter irate like this. Normally, he was the more levelheaded one, and Gerasimou was most likely to fly off the handle.

Having him lose control like this did everything for my libido, and I was ready to drop to my knees to allow him to use my throat for penance.

We stayed like that, faces so close we breathed each other's air, until there was a knock at the door, pulling all three of our attention to it.

Gerasimou opened it to find Hanna, Hans' daughter. "Hallo. Mr. Finlay asked that I come and get you three to come to his chambers immediately."

Gerasimou looked to Carter, and then they both looked to me, and I felt it in my soul that Finlay found something we could go off of.

Carter assisted me to stand from where I was haphazardly thrown on the bed, before he placed a kiss on my nose and then Gerasimou to my temple.

Together, we rushed out of the room to Finlay's with my heart in my throat and stomach in my ass; the whole time, praying that it was something we could use.

G

Fucking finally! I thought as we walked throughout the ridiculously large manor to Fin's room. He had been taking more time than he should to get any information on the whereabouts of our kids.

I had already decided that if he didn't have anything by tonight, I was gonna knock his fucking eyes into the 20/20 range so then maybe he would have the ability see what the fuck he should be doing better.

Lykáki held onto my arm tightly as we walked. I glanced down to find her chewing her bottom lip. Gently, in a way I only possessed with her, I used my thumb to relieve her assault on it.

Her eyes shot up to mine, worry lines marring her beautiful face. Her freckles that I'd memorized down to the cluster over the bridge of her nose, pulled my attention from her hazel green eyes. Transfixed on them, I had the sudden urge to want to trace each and every one of the ones on her face down to the ones that peppered her delectable body.

"Gerasimou," she called out to me.

"Hmm..." I answered reluctantly.

"I really hope Finlay found something useful," she stated.

Her words did its job to bring my attention back to the present and not on more salacious acts my mind began to conjure up. It also reminded me that we had yet to tell her what he had already found.

Earlier when we had gone to look for her to tell her what he found, we found her gone. If it wasn't for the necklace she wore and Ivor letting us know, we would have thought that fucker Javier grew bigger balls and came on the Davis property to take her.

"Hey," I said, halting my steps. Since she was holding on to my arm, she also stopped. "What did we tell you?"

Carter had now stopped on the other side of her as he was walking right behind us. She looked to him then back at me. The hesitant and skeptical glint in her eyes was morphing to confidence as she must have been playing our words back in her mind.

It wasn't enough to see that she remembered; I needed to hear her speak it aloud. "No, *Lykáki*, your words," I spoke to her in my native language.

"That you will find them, the both of you. And bring them back home to me." She repeated the words we had said to her many times over the last four days.

"Do you believe we will?" I asked her, lifting her head high with the knuckle of my index finger.

Her eyes shone bright with the blind trust she had in us, even though truthfully, we hadn't earned it from her, nor did we deserve it.

She didn't say anything at first. She seemed lost in our stare, like she was searching for the reason she believed a word I spoke, or maybe she was looking deeper and seeing something I didn't want her to.

Thankfully, Carter spoke and broke the trance we both were under. " *Yume*..." She turned and looked at him. I knew the same way she showed her trust in me, she showed him. "There isn't a thing in this world we would allow to stop us from getting our children back to you unharmed. If it took our last breath to fulfill this promise to you, we would happily give it."

Carter's eyes shifted over Lorelei's head to mine. We held each other's stare locking in the promise he spoke to her, to each other.

However, I had no intention to make sure that we, along with our children, were the last ones standing at the end of this.

Without prompt, all three of us continued the walk to Fin's, allowing the silence to prepare us for whatever the fuck he was about to show or tell us. When we approached the door, Carter turned to Lorelei. She looked up to him, eyebrows knitted as she waited for his reason for why we stopped.

"*Yume*, whatever Fin shows us in there, remember that it doesn't matter. It doesn't change the outcome of how we will move or what we will do for our children. Do not allow it to break you. Do not allow it to sway you from the trust you have in us. Do not lose faith!"

He said that shit with so much reverence that even though I knew there wasn't a chance in hell that anything was going to stop me, his words gave me a confidence boost.

"I believe you both will do whatever it takes. I trust that you will bring them home." *Lykáki* gave him a small smile before she rose to her toes and placed a kiss to his lips. She then turned to me and gave me one as well.

We were close to the part of the house where Fin was, when my phone buzzed distinctively in my pocket with an incoming call. Pulling it out, I saw that it was Riker.

"I gotta take this," I said to them both.

Carter knew the vibration and who was on the other line. *Lykáki* didn't but still gave me the privacy needed to take the call.

"Do they know?" Carter asked before following behind Lorelei.

I nodded. I had told Skip, who was Riker's brother and second in command, what was going on when it first happened. I hoped with the ties the *Iron Saints* had to the criminal underground, they might have heard or would have heard something to help us.

"Yo," I answered.

"Brother," Riker greeted.

"You got something for me?" I asked him, cutting right to the chase.

"I see we're cutting pleasantries." He chuckled. Normally, I would indulge with him, but this wasn't the time.

"Riker, I don't have time for your bullshit!" I snapped. "If you got something, tell me, man."

"Alright, man, damn," he conceded. "Smalls got word from this hopper he was takin' down. She said her sister who messes with this cat from the Raisin' Sons overheard that there was some new product on the market. She continued to listen, and they revealed it was something rare and that you had to have top money for it.

"She didn't know they were into that sick shit. But as soon as she learned that they had confirmation it was bodies they were sellin', she ain't want any parts in it. The only reason she told her sister was because she wanted her to get her into Iron Saints and figured she could give us this info for good measure."

Riker said shit we already knew except the confirmation. "How the fuck they confirmed it was bodies?"

"Oh..." I could hear the smile in his voice. "We grabbed the fucker, and Kilt made him squawk. Apparently, these fuckers have an in with the Giraldo Cartel. We are still working him over for details, but...there is a site. It had a countdown, but by time we got in there, it was just about to end, and man.. the shit on there. Two little fucking kids, man, about the same age. They look nothing alike but do, so they gotta be twins; I don't know, man. That shit ain't even relevant to saving them. Whatever you need, you know we got your back, Brother."

Anger coursed through me knowing he was describing our kids. When I told him about the shit going down, I didn't tell him all the details. But hearing how pissed and on go he was to help get them solidified how much they rolled with me.

"Appreciate it, Brother," I thanked him. "If we need you, I'll for sure reach out."

"You know we rock with you the long way, Dimitri. You may have switched to the big leagues with that big ass Viking, but you will always be an Iron Saint. Step on Iron..."

"Feel the burn." I finished our club's tag, ending the call.

That fucker Javier surely stepped on the wrong fucking iron, and I was gonna make sure he felt that shit.

Carter

"What do you have, Fin?" I asked them the moment we all stepped into his room, after G finished his call with Riker.

"Aye, lads, I got intel on the twins," he said, turning in his large desk chair to face us. *Yume*'s face lit up with excitement at finding them. "However, the timer ended, and it revealed that my suspicions were correct."

"I just got off the phone with Riker. He told me they got confirmation too. But that's all he had."

"Wait, site? What site? And a timer? What suspicion?" She rapidly fired question after question. Panic set in her voice.

Shit! I forgot that I was supposed to tell her not only what Fin found but about my conversation with Claro.

Turning to her, I took her hands in mine. I knew that her hearing what the site was for would most likely send her into hysteria. "*Yume*... Fin's intel sent him a website earlier that had a timer on it. I am assuming now that the timer has completed, we now know what is being sold on the site."

Her breath hitched, eyes going wide. They glossed with unshed tears, but she didn't allow them to fall. Instead, she looked up to the ceiling, taking in deep breaths for a few moments before she lowered her gaze to me.

Pride swelled in my chest when all I could see was determination. Giving me a shaky smile, she gave Fin her attention. "Can we see the site?" she asked.

Fin looked at me and then G. We both nodded because we too hadn't seen what was on the site. After a few clicks, the site was pulled up on the main screen–our twins' faces in two individual photos.

"If you click them," Fin said, clicking the photo of Wolfe first, "there is an album of different photos of them."

He went through Wolfe's photos then did the same for Dream. Then clicked on a conjoined album with photos of them together.

"Stop," *Yume* whispered, but it was loud enough for us all to hear. "Please, I can't see anymore."

She was hugging herself as G pulled her tightly into his chest. "What is the time frame?" he asked.

"The auction starts in thirty-six hours. That was all the information given," he answered.

My phone buzzed in my pants. Brows furrowed, I pulled it out. When I saw the number I used to call Claro, my heartbeat accelerated. I gave her forty-eight hours six hours ago and hadn't expected to hear from her this soon.

My eyes shot to G, and his were already on mine. He nodded to it as if telling me to answer it. I looked over to Fin as well. I had told them both about my call with her earlier, so they knew we were waiting for this call.

Sliding my thumb across the screen, I placed the phone to my ear. Silently, I waited for her to speak, refusing to speak first.

"Javone," she spoke carefully, almost like she was approaching a predatory animal.

I didn't speak. She called me, so she knew who she was talking to.

"Do you really hate me, *hijo*?" she asked, having the audacity to sound hurt.

"Claro," I said coldly.

"I know, I know. I just..." She let out a deep sigh. "Javier isn't taking my calls, but I know where he is holding them and the nanny. My inside person let me know the twins are okay. They have been telling them they are on a trip to meet their *abuelita*. I have plans to fly out with your father in a–"

"My father?!" I boomed. Lorelei jumped at the sound of my voice, concern filled her eyes.

I never raised my voice in her presence before. It wasn't something I wanted her to associate me with. Unfortunately, the normal ability I had to control my emotions were nonexistent at this point.

"Look, I don't know what fucking sick shit you and my father have going on, Claro. I truly do not give a fuck. All I want to know is the location of my children. You have seven seconds to tell me, or I will rip it from your fucking throat." I gritted.

"They are in Berlin. They are staying in a Citadel Hotel. He is checked in under Jason Crowne," she reluctantly spoke. "And whether you believe me or not, your father and I care and love you more than you know, Javone. And we love our grandchildren."

I didn't even dignify her words with a response. I hung up the call and met the eyes of G and *Yume*, each of their looks meaning something different.

G's were understanding while Lorelei's were a mix of confusion and empathy. I had to close my eyes and take a deep breath to calm myself. I couldn't allow my parentage to cloud my mind, preventing me from doing what needed to be to bring our children home.

"Fin," I said, calmer than I felt.

"Aye?" he answered.

"Reach out to Ayela. Ask her to check with the Citadel in Berlin under Jason Crowne." I saw *Yume* stiffen at the name. "I know the protocol and that they aren't allowed to disclose who their guest are, but I don't give a fuck. Find out."

Fin paused a moment before he recovered and got to business. I turned to Lorelei and G next.

I could tell she had questions, and as much as I'd rather not, I knew I had to answer them.

"Who was that?" she asked, stroking my cheek.

I closed my eyes and took a deep breath before answering. "My mother."

She shook her head and blinked a few times before she collected herself. "Your mother?" she asked slowly, almost like she was saying more than the two words.

"*Hai*."

Nodding her head, she pulled in her lips then released them into a purse. "Your mother took my fucking kids?!"

"As far as we know, no. She didn't, but..." I paused.

"What, Carter?!" she demanded. "But what?"

"Javier is my brother," I reluctantly answered.

"This is fucking great. I have been feeling guilty thinking it was something I did, but it was because of you." She pointed in my face. Then she turned to G. "And you knew about this and told me nothing?"

"It wasn't like that, *Lykáki*," G defended. "This shit is complicated. But that ain't change a damn thing when it comes to us doing what the fuck we need to get them back, you feel me?"

She studied both of our faces like she was searching for the truth. I hated to bring anything but pleasure or joy to her. Seeing that she had tears running down her face, messed with my brain. Taking her face into my hands, I wiped them away with the pads of my thumb. It was exactly what I would always do for her–wipe her tears and right any wrongs done in her life.

"Do you trust us?" I asked her.

Without hesitation, she nodded her head.

G came to my side pulling her attention. "Then now we got you. Them. Us."

Yume gave us a small smile despite the tears that still cascaded down her freckled cheeks. I softly kissed her lips, G doing the same after.

Once I felt she was okay, I turned to Fin and asked, "You think Henrik will allow us to use his jet?"

Fin shook his head knowing Henrik was going to give us hell for asking for his plane. But at this point, I would take it regardless to get our kids.

"Shit, I hope. It's the only thing big enough to carry us and The Saints," G added.

"Ach, you lads pulled the Iron Saints to join ya." Fin chuckled. "Well, I guess we're going to Berlin."

Lorelei

I was fucking livid.

After leaving Finaly's room, we came back to ours. I couldn't lie nor hide that I was beaming from the promise of getting my babies back. Not just with sweet words either, but with an actual time and plans.

What pissed me off was when we got to the room, Carter let me know I wouldn't be going.

"What do you mean I'm not going?" I asked.

"Yume, we do not know what we are walking into. You going would mean a distraction neither of us need. Not when the price of the well being of our children are on the line," he said with finality.

I laughed, but there was no humor behind it. "So, you expect me to fucking sit here and wait for you to possibly get my kids back to me? Is that what you're telling me?"

"Lorelei..." he said my name with exasperation.

"Do not fucking Lorelei me. I'm coming, end of story," I spat.

Gerasimou didn't say anything, he was too busy texting whoever on his phone, but I could also tell he paid attention to Carter and I going back and forth about me going. I was standing ten toes down on them not leaving me, but Carter...Carter had me ready to gouge his fucking eyes out.

At that point, we were screaming at each other, my anger boiling to the point it felt like steam was spilling from my ears.

A knock coming to the door was the only thing that stopped us from continuing. When G opened it, Hanna stood there with that fucking stupid ass smile she permanently wore. The moment she noticed it was Gerasimou, her pale cheeks turned crimson as she stuttered to speak.

"Umm... gud day. My father has sent me to collect you and Carter. Henrik would like to speak with you." She could barely hold his gaze.

"Thank you, Hanna, we will be there shortly," he responded.

Gerasimou wasn't a man who spoke a lot unless he needed to, and I felt they didn't need to say more than a head nod to this woman. Without thinking, I was at the door trying to snatch the bitch through the door.

"Yume!"

"Lykáki!"

They yelled in unison.

I ignored them trying to get at her. However, large hands pulled me back into the room and then shut the door.

Carter lifted me off the floor before he haphazardly threw me onto the bed like Gerasimou had earlier.

I tried to rise again, fury still snapping in my veins, but Carter pushed me right back down.

"Calm the fuck down, Lorelei!" he thundered.

And just like that girl in the video saying I'm sat?

I was sat.

Fuming.

Boiling.

Ready to light the whole damn manor up behind that pale little twinkle-smiling bitch.

How dare she flirt with Gerasimou right in front of me?

Better question:

How the hell did he let her?

"We know emotions are high, Yume. But the decision is final. We'll be back before we leave, but right now, we need to debrief."

Carter kissed me chastely, and Gerasimou followed but gentler. Their switch in tenderness had my head spinning.

Now I sat here pissed beyond reason that they were leaving me out of getting our children back. How did they expect me just to sit here twiddling my thumbs?

I barely made it five minutes staring at the ceiling before I felt like I was going stir crazy. My stomach growling was the push I needed to get out of this room before I lost it.

Almost to the kitchen, I started hearing laughter and chatter. Once I rounded the corner, I found Saysha, Faven, and Deidre sitting at the dining nook talking to each other, eating dinner. Faven had one twin in her arms, while Deidre had the other.

A smile came to my face despite how annoyed I still felt. Saysha was the first to notice me. A mischievous smile crossed her face causing my brows to furrow and my eyes to shift to the side.

"Uh… hi," I said, walking closer to them.

"Hi my ass, girl," Faven sassed with humor lacing her tone.

"Leave her be," Deidre murmured, brushing a thumb over the twin's cheek. "She's had a testing few days."

Saysha snorted. "Yeah, an evening where she tried to choke Hanna out in the hallway."

My head snapped in her direction. "I did not—"

"She said you grabbed her arm, girl." Saysha held up both hands. "I'm just reporting what the victim claims."

Faven let out a quiet laugh, low and dangerous, bouncing one of her newborn twins absently. "Hanna isn't one to run her mouth. I'm sure you barely touched her. But Lord, the way she was screeching? Sounded like someone clipped her wings."

"I didn't even touch her. Carter scooped me before I got too close," I muttered, jaw tight. "But if it wasn't for him, I most likely would have."

"Why did you anyway?" Deidre asked.

Finally I sat down at the table with the ladies. "Because she is always so damn smiley."

"Ohhhhh..." they all said in unison.

"What?" I asked.

"Girl, she must have been smiling in either thing one or two's face then, 'cause baby, based off the way that girl ran in here..." Saysha chortled.

"I'm actually surprised," Faven added.

"Surprised?" I asked.

"Yeah, you know Hans is her father, right?" Faven looked at me perplexed.

"I mean, no one told me, but I put two and two together."

"Well, Hans is more than just our house manager. That man used to be a deadly assassin way back when," Faven informed us. "I'm surprised she ran in here scared because there's no way her father didn't teach her how to defend herself."

I shrugged my shoulders, not really caring to dissect whatever her too friendly ass could and couldn't do.

"You okay?" Faven asked. She was now nursing both babies.

I was proud of how well she adapted to motherhood and nursing not just one but two babies. The soft gulps and coos that spilled from the tiny blessing dulled the ache for my babies a bit.

"Yeah," I said, giving her a small smile.

"You're not. Let me guess, the boys told you you couldn't go?" she inquired. But I could tell by her smirk she already knew the answer.

"Told her she can't go where?" Saysha snapped.

"It's fine, I understand their reasoning. Do I agree? No. But that is just because I need to be there," I huffed.

"Wait, did things one and two tell you that you couldn't go with them to get your kids back?" Saysha gasped, shock evident on her face. "I know you ain't tellin' me that right now."

Deidre laughed. And as it seems with everyone in this world of ours, the laugh wasn't filled with humor. "That's cute. He thinks he can tell you what you can and can't do. Especially when it comes to your children. I think the fuck not."

She stood up from the table abruptly, slamming her palm on it in the process. This was the first time I'd ever heard Deidre in any tone that wasn't pleasantly controlled . From what I remember of us as kids, she was usually the peacemaker of the bunch. So, this side of her was entertaining in the best way.

Saysha stood up next with an impish smile spread wide on her face. "So, clearly if they don't want you to go, it's because they want *us* to go..." She rubbed her hands together giggling wickedly. "I haven't caused mischief in Berlin in *years*!"

We all broke into laughter. "Who's going to Berlin?"

Everyone turned. Soleil appeared in the doorway of the kitchen, arms crossed, her golden sister locs swinging softly.

Saysha jerked a thumb at me. "We are. Since the boys weren't gonna take your sister, we're gonna crash their ride there."

Soleil's eyes narrowed, dark and unreadable. "Why?"

"Because they think I'll be a distraction or in the way," I whispered.

"No," Soleil corrected in her flat, melodic way. "Because they underestimate you. What's worse is that not only are you letting them, but you're underestimating yourself."

One of the babies in Faven's arms made a soft sound while the other still ate, and she adjusted her on her shoulder, her face shadowed by thought. "They're idiots," she said simply. "Every last one, and if Henrik allows them to, he clearly didn't learn shit from the last time."

Deidre let out a quiet hum—the kind she made right before suggesting something deranged and wildly effective. "Well," she said, "like I said. If they want to leave without us... we don't let them."

Soleil's lips curled into the barest hint of a smile. "I haven't had a good trip in a while," she mused. "Sounds interesting."

Faven raised one brow. "You have an idea?"

Deidre nodded, serene as a saint with blood on her hem. "The private hangar is close. We get in, stay out of sight, and wait. Let them think they're leaving us behind until the doors close."

Saysha grinned. "Like stowaways. But sexy."

Soleil shrugged. "Or armed."

My pulse kicked, heat sliding into my chest. "Y'all would really do that?"

Saysha leaned back, she now held one of Faven's babies snug against her shoulder, her voice quiet and absolute. "For you? For those babies? Always."

Deidre slapped her hands on the table. "Alright then. Let's ruin their whole plan. Pack light. Move fast."

And Soleil, already turning toward the hall, spoke without looking back. "And wear black."

G

The plan was simple. Me, Carter, Banks, Ivor, a few members of the Iron Saints, and Fin were gonna use Henrik's plane and get to Berlin.

When we got there, Ayela was going to have a suite ready for us that we could enter through a private entrance. As far as we knew, Javier wasn't staying there. Ayela checked their surveillance system, and neither him nor his alias were listed. We also checked the cameras for facial recognition, and nothing came up, but we knew from Riker and Carter's mom, they were indeed in Berlin.

Everything happened so damn fast we didn't even get a chance to tell *Lykáki* we were leaving. Faven promised she'd handle it. And since she was asleep... yeah. That made it easier. I preferred it, if I was being real.

Facing her would've slowed us down. She would've argued, cussed, and threatened to come with us. And I couldn't afford any of that—not with the clock chewing through our time.

Riker and a few of the Iron Saints were already headed to Ithaca, non-surprisingly, when he called. Told Henrik, when he called him, they'd meet us at the plane. *Good*. We needed everybody we trusted on this run.

Henrik's jet sat there waiting as we pulled, looking like a sleek death bringer that it was. Every time I saw it, it messed with my head a little. If somebody had told me as a kid that I'd be rolling with men who owned their own planes, I'd have laughed in their face. Probably swung on them too.

My life used to be nothing but ruin. I didn't see a future—hell, I barely saw a point. The only positive I could picture was my death, and even that felt like a long shot.

When I met Carter... like I said before, that uptight fucker changed my life.

Then I met *Lykáki*. *My gods*, that changed the rest. Changed my heart, my spine, my damn blood. Suddenly, I had two kids who needed me–two little lives I'd die for without thinking.

And a woman who made me want to live long enough to come back home.

The time it took us to park, get our bags, and talk with the pilot. Riker and the crew were pulling up. I made the introductions to Fin, Ivor, and Banks before we boarded the plane.

Very few things in my thirty-four years of life surprised me. I'd seen so much shit that I expected the unexpected as remedial as that sounded.

What I wasn't prepared for was to find my *Lykáki*, her sister, Saysha and Deidre fucking Davis to be sitting on their asses on Henrik's plane like we invited their asses.

"Red!" Ivor's voice boomed over all of us.

"Big, don't say nothin' ta me. You a whole damn headache, ya heard?" She fired off back to him, her Louisiana accent thicker than I'd ever heard it. "You really thought you was gon' dip out an' leave me? Nawl, miss me wit' that." She sucked her teeth, a sharp *tuh* cutting the air. "Go 'head an' park y'all asses. This gon' be a long-ass nine-hour flight."

Riker and his guys laughed, taking a seat introducing themselves. Ivor and Saysha started bickering, while Fin went to talk with Deidre, who didn't seem surprised that the ladies were here. *Fucking brown-noser.*

Carter and I stood in front of a very smug and pissed off Lorelei. Carter was equally pissed while I, surprised, was turned on that she snuck her beautiful ass on this plane, despite the fact we told her she couldn't.

Truthfully, I didn't care if she came, but it was more so I didn't want to be that far away from her for that long. I agreed that it wasn't for the best she came when we got the twins back, but I also didn't think she was incapable of handling herself if given the chance.

Carter didn't utter a word to her, he just walked over to her and grabbed her arm, taking her to the back bedroom with me following closely behind them. Her sister jumped up to say something, but I stopped her.

I knew Carter enough to know he wasn't going to hurt *Lykáki*. Just like I knew he only was bringing her back to that room because he didn't like showing his emotions in front of people.

When I entered, they were staring at each other hard. You could see the heat radiating from their skin. Lorelei whipped her head in my direction, directing her ire towards me.

"Woah," I said, holding my hands up in surrender. "I know you're pissed, *Lykáki*.

"Pissed," she chortled. "You think I'm pissed, Gerasimou? Try fucking livid!"

"Yes, pissed, and you have every right to be." Carter threw daggers at me with his eyes, but I didn't give a shit. She did have a right to be pissed. "She does, C, and you know it."

"So, I'm the bad guy because I want to keep her safe?" Carter asked, devoid of any emotion, and I knew right then that meant he was seconds from losing it.

"You know that's not—" my words were cut off by Lorelei.

"That's exactly what the fuck I'm saying." She pushed at his chest, but he didn't move. "You both run around here like you're some super fucking saviors. You stormed into my life, integrated yourselves, made me fucking love you both, then you leave me alone for four fucking years to raise our babies, then because of you...both of you, they are taken, and you want me to do nothing? To sit there all pretty why you galivant across the globes in hopes you get them to me safe all while you stop some fucking psychopath with a vendetta?

"So, to answer your question, Carter. If you stand in my way of getting *my* kids back, then yes, you are the bad guy." She stepped even closer to him. "And if either of you try to stand in my way, I will fucking destroy you from your mind to your fucking body."

With that, she stormed out of the room back to the main part of the plane. And if her flipping out like that, threatening bodily harm and then switching her voluptuous ass out of here, wasn't the sexiest thing I'd ever seen.

"Fuck! She is a vision," I murmured.

"That she is, brother," Carter agreed. "That she is."

Carter

I stood in the bedroom long after G left. All the information presented to me over the last few days filtered through my mind. *Speaking to Claro. Javier is my brother. My father reaching out to me. Learning I was a father. Seeing* Yume *again.*

I ran my hand through my curls. *Yume*. My *Yume-chan*. My dream. I'd known I would see her again, but I didn't expect it to be on the terms laid before us.

At first, I thought I was dreaming when we went to get the midwife, seeing her standing in the foyer. The moment our eyes met, the obsession that had been lying dormant in me, came rushing back.

Then being told that I was a father at the same time my children had been stolen, knocked the air out of my chest. Not to mention the person who did it, I unknowingly shared blood with.

Kuso! I needed to get my mind together. I was losing it.

Losing control.

I didn't lose control.

But this shit was testing every single thing I knew about myself. Every single thing I prided myself on.

And for the fucking life of me I couldn't determine if it was a good thing or not. What I did know was that I didn't have the time right now to analyze it either. I needed to be that controlled and calculated assassin I was bred to be.

My kids' lives depended on it. *Yume*'s sanity depended on it. And G, no, Dimitri's heart, depended on it.

I saw the changes having her here and knowing about our kids had on him. The calmer he had been, despite the circumstances. The way he spoke more.

That was all I wanted for my brother was for him to get out of his head and his trauma.

A knock came at the door and opened before I could say anything. Solelei walked in with an unreadable look on her face.

I hadn't known Solelei for long, we met her a few years back when she was brought in to break Darryl Davis. Our interactions were limited, but there was always something about her—something that drew attention, that demanded notice. G noticed it too. He remarked how much she reminded him of Lorelei, and I could only shake my head at our own blindness. Of course she was Yume's sister. It had been staring us in the face.

They weren't identical. Solelei's complexion was darker, but the structure was the same: full lips, freckles, hazel eyes. Yume wore her hair in locs; while Solelei preferred natural curls or braids. Subtle differences, but the same blood running through them.

I hadn't given any other woman even a thought since Lorelei. None had stirred me, none had reached inside and reshaped me the way she had. The way she awakened something I didn't know I possessed, set it alight. It was singular. Her taste, her scent, the way she existed in the world, it was hers alone. No one else could ever come close. And I hadn't allowed them to. Not since the last time I took her.

Fingers snapped in my face, pulling my attention from my *Yume-chan*. "Hello. Do you hear me talking to you?"

I narrowed my eyes at Solelei. While I never put my hands on a woman, I couldn't help but visualize me snapping her slender neck for blatant disrespect. "What is it that you want, Solelei?" I asked her.

She returned my glare with one of her own. "Listen to me, you robot." *Hmm…robot, that was a new assessment.* "I do not give a damn about what the fuck it is you do as a profession, but I do not play about my sister. She has been through a lot in the last four years. If either of you do anything to upset her more than she already is… I'll make what I did to Darryl look like child's play."

She didn't wait for my response, just slipped out as fast as she entered, leaving me to shake my head. This was going to be a long nine hours.

When I entered the plane, everyone was seated already.

Fin and Banks sat towards the back near the bedroom I just left, across from two of the men who came with Riker. G was across from Riker and Smalls in another seating area. I looked up in the middle of the plane where the women sat.

Yume sat next to her sister with Deidre and Saysha across from her. Ivor, of course, sat towards the front where he could see Saysha.

I studied *Yume*, watching her talk with the women. Her ire still evident from our conversation. Although it bothered me that she was so upset, I knew there wasn't much I could do about it right now. I stood on the fact I didn't want her to accompany us to Berlin.

Unfortunately with the time wasted already, I didn't have any left to fight with not only her but the rest of the women and Ivor. Because Ivor was going to react to anything that negatively impacted Saysha. I couldn't fault him. G and I would be, *are*, the same way for Lorelei.

Collecting myself, I sat, in perfect view of Yume, in the empty seat next to G. He was already in a conversation with Riker and Smalls.

"Still looks like we gotta bail ya out, kid," Smalls jested.

G smiled slightly. "Never. You better watch your old ass knees, *aderfós*."

Riker looked up to me. "That's mama bear?" he asked, jutting his head back in *Yume's* direction.

I lifted my head to see her looking in our direction. Her face was unreadable, but I saw the fire in her eyes. Like she was daring me to try and remove her from this plane.

I shook my head, more at myself than her, refocusing my attention back to Riker. "*Hai*," I answered.

He grinned at us both. "You two would be the stupid motherfuckers who fall in love with the same girl. Then go and have a damn phenomenon of children. Still can't do shit with the other I see."

Needing to lighten the mood, I joined Riker's joking. "What would be the fun in that?"

"Shit, I just want to know how you fuckers make that work with her." Smalls butted in. His statement was met with a slap to the back of the head.

"What?!" he exclaimed. "So, what, only you can joke? Damn."

"Would you like someone asking you how you take down ya old lady, idgit?" Riker asked him.

"I'd have to take these broads serious to have an old lady first, Rike." Smalls shrugged.

Riker just shook at him.

I didn't take any offense to what Smalls said. I'd known these men long enough to know it was never nothing malicious between us. Smalls didn't have a filter, much like Saysha.

Rheda, the flight attendant, stepped into the cabin and delivered a polished welcome, outlining our overnight flight to Germany and confirming we were cleared for takeoff. The flight would run just under nine hours.

Seatbelts clicked into place around us. Within minutes, the engines roared to life, and we were ascending into the dark.

After we reached cruising altitude, Rheda returned with a cart of light refreshments, quietly offering drinks and snacks before reminding us that meals would be available throughout the flight and breakfast served before landing.

"Damn, Lo, why you had to try and beat up Hanna for?" Saysha gripped. "She gives the good shit. This chick acting like the peanuts coming from her check or something."

This caused almost everyone to laugh. I was still as was *Yume* as she watched me.

After the first couple of hours of the flight, everyone was either asleep or moved about the plane in different locations. Fin was on his laptop, doing who knows what. Saysha was asleep practically in Ivor's lap while he laid back in his seat.

Solelei had gone to one of the bedrooms to get sleep, and Yume was now seated closer to the back playing a game of cards with Smalls. The rest were either asleep or working.

"How is it you keep beating me in *Uno*?" Lorelei complained lowly

"Because I know how to play, little one," Smalls answered playfully. "I can show you how to play if you want to."

"Are you flirting with me, Smalls?" *Yume* asked him.

Smalls chuckled. "So, Dimitri can show me how my gallbladder works on the outside? I think not little one."

I could see how she would think Smalls was flirting with her however, this wasn't him flirting. He was treating her more like a sister.

Smalls didn't exactly flirt, he made innuendos that let you know exactly what he wanted.

Yume furrowed her brows. "Dimitri?"

Smalls nodded his head towards Where G had moved to talk with Banks.

"Wait, are you talking about Gerasimou? His name isn't Dimitri." She stated with confidence.

Smalls tilted his head to the side, sticking his tongue in his cheek. Studying her before he broke out into a loud laugh. "No way," He leaned to the side, catching G's attention. "Hey fuck hat. You been doing the three's company with your old lady, and she don't know your first name?!"

"His first name?" *Yume* glanced my way, confusion written all over her face.

G left where we was and made his way over to us, sitting next to Smalls. *Yume* lifted her head in his direction. "I thought your name was Gerasimou."

"It is." Was his response. "My last name.

Saysha was now sitting up in Ivor's lap. "Oh you really the goat. Took down these two statues, gave them two babies, all without knowing their first names. Guhl, I want to be like you when I grow up." She did a little dance in Ivor's lap with her tongue out.

"Red..." he warned.

"Only with you, Big." She turned and kissed him chastely on the lips.

Yume stood from her seat, abruptly. "Can I speak with you? Both of you."

G looked over to me, annoyance on his face that I was sure mirrored mine as she walked back to the room a few feet away.

I could already feel a headache blooming.

G

"I know that there are a million things that could be bothering me right now." *Lykáki* started the moment we walked through the door, pacing the floor. "I could be stressing about if my kids are ok—"

"Our," Carter said plainly. "Our kids."

Her head whipped in his direction. "At this fucking very moment, do not piss me off, Carter. Or whatever your damn name is." She gritted.

"Javone. My first name is Javone, *Yume*."

She scoffed. "Just fucking great."

"Lorelei..." I dragged. I really wasn't in the mood for her theatrics.

I'd been allowing her to make it with her inconsistent mood swings, giving all that'd been going on, but at the moment, I was seconds from showing her that I wasn't the man to push.

"Tuh, please, *Dimitri*." She dragged out the pronunciation of my name while holding her hand up, dismissing me.

Why was that the thing that sent me over the edge? I didn't know. Either way it did, and before she could blink, I had her pinned against the wall.

"You know, *Lykáki*... I'm going to blame that disrespect on the stress you're under."

My voice stayed low... even–too even.

She knew that tone. It was the one I used on her in that cabin all those years ago.

I kept my eyes on hers. Didn't blink. Didn't soften. "But hear me now. My mind isn't wired right all the time. You push me with that little attitude of yours, and I'm going to answer in a way you're not ready for."

Her breath stuttered. She tried to hide it, but I caught the way her chest rose faster, the way her throat worked when she swallowed.

The anger from earlier didn't disappear. It changed shape.

It became something warmer and darker, strung between us like a tripwire waiting to snap.

Her fingers flexed like she wanted to reach for me and fight me at the same time.

She stared back without backing down, and that alone lit something feral under my ribs.

I leaned in closer. My voice barely above a whisper. I wanted her to feel more than she heard me.

"*Lykáki*..." I growled, my hand moving to her neck. "You like that, don't you? Maybe that's what it is you need. C, I think that's her problem."

I looked over my shoulder to see Carter already moving closer, slow and measured, like a tiger stalking prey before the strike.

Licking his lip slowly, he came to her side, lowering his face into the crook of her neck. He inhaled, dragging his nose up the side of her neck until he was at the lobe of her ear.

"Is that what is the matter, *Yume*? Are you so out of sorts you are in need of us to right you?" he whispered, but I heard him.

"I... I don't know what you're talking about," she sputtered breathlessly.

"Oh, but I think you do, little wolf." I was now at her other ear, allowing my breath to feather it.

She shivered involuntarily, and it told us everything she was trying to deny. All the reasons she held that anger so tightly in her grip was warranted. Her body, though?

Gods, her fucking delectable body needed us.

My body pressed into hers just enough to let her know she had nowhere to run. Her scent hit me like a punch, sweet and warm, drawing out the part of me that always slipped whenever she pushed too far.

It rolled off her in waves, and I knew Carter smelled it too.

"You can deny it all you want, *Yume*," Carter said. His voice brushed her skin. "Your body already told the truth."

She inhaled deeply, her chest rose as she held my gaze. Her pupils were blown with desire just that quick.

She tried to hold herself together, but that little tremble in her lip gave her away.

I brought my hand to her waist and kept it just clean enough to deny. My palm settled on her hip, close enough to ruin her concentration and feel her muscles tighten.

I leaned in until my lips hovered a breath from hers.

"You feel that," I murmured. "Every inch of you wants to give in. You think we can't tell?"

She pulled her plump bottom lip between her teeth as if she could ward the feeling we were giving her away.

Carter kissed the side of her neck, slow and deliberate. Her whole body reacted. I felt the shift of her weight. The way her breathing stuttered. The way her hands pressed against my chest, not to push me away, but because she needed something to hold on.

I lifted her chin. Forced her to look at me. Her eyes darted down to where my hand was, then to the side where Carter was now licking his way to her ear. Her bottom lip shook like she was fighting something inside herself.

Without saying, we lifted her shirt up and over her head. Reluctantly breaking the contact our lips had with her. We brushed our hands on the outside of the full coverage bra she wore.

Her breath caught. She swallowed audibly, like her throat had gone dry and we were the only thing to quench the thirst building there.

"Tell us what you want, *moró mou*." My lips brushed her ear as I spoke.

"Let us what you need, *anata*," Carter murmured against her ear as we toyed with her nipples through her bra, leaving her writhing between our bodies and the wall with nowhere to go.

"Please," she begged, but I was sure she couldn't even tell us for what.

I kissed the spot right under her chin, and Carter took her lips with his in a sensual kiss. We alternated between me at her neck and Carter at her lips, then me at her lips and Carter at neck until she moaned and bucked the lower half of her body like she was hoping to brush it with a part of us.

"You need us, *Lykáki*?" I asked her, licking my lips to catch the taste of her again.

She nodded feverishly.

"You want us, *Yume*?" Her eyes flickered to Carter's as she nodded again.

I laughed low and dark. "Look at you, baby. So fucking ready for us. I bet you've been thinking about it, haven't you?"

Carter smiled slyly, picking up where I left off. "Thought about how we owned your body. How we slipped into all your holes and marked you as ours."

We dipped our hands in her pants and past her panties. My finger brushed past her ball of nerves until I reached that greedy entrance that I could feel contracting. Carter's hand went to her throbbing clit massaging it.

Lykáki's mouth fell open in a silent cry that Carter silenced with a kiss. Needing to taste a part of her, I pulled the cup of her bra down exposing her taunt nipple, pulling it into my mouth.

"Fuckkkk..." she groaned, lacing her hand through my hair. "Please don't stop."

And we didn't, we continued switching who did what to bring her to the brink of pleasure. My dick strained at my slacks, begging to sink in its home for the first time in four years.

But once she came down from our assault, Carter grabbed her a warm rag to clean between her legs. We straightened her clothes then each gave her a long kiss that dared to heat us all over.

She looked at us sheepishly but with a flame of desire still lingering in her beautiful hazel brown eyes. I lifted her chin up to focus solely on me.

"The next time you need us to adjust your mood, just ask, *Lykáki*."

Carter used my hand to turn her to face him. "There is no need to act out." He paused like he was thinking, tilting his head to sell it. "Or do. We are fine with either."

I slapped her ass, adjusted my still-hardened dick, and headed back to the main cabin with Carter right behind me.

Lorelei

My legs were still shaking when I finally mustered up the courage to leave the bedroom. I prayed like hell that it was soundproof, so no one heard my begs or what it sounded like when I orgasm. It blew my mind how perfectly they were able to not only individually take my body to new heights, but to do so together, without uttering a word to each other.

Carter and Gerasimou were now seated on the sofa that sat in the middle of the plane on the left. Not even thinking about it, almost like it was something pulling me towards them, I sat between them.

Gerasimou bent to grab my feet, pulling them into his lap, while Carter laid my head in his lap.

"You okay, *Yume*? " Carter asked as he kissed my forehead.

"Mhm," I mumbled, snuggling into him. "I'm okay, *Javone*."

Gerasimou laughed as he removed my sneakers and began massaging my feet. I let out a soft moan with how good it felt.

"Is there something funny, *Dimitri*?" I taunted, a slick smile on my lips.

I could feel Carter releasing the clip of the elastic band, my locs cascading to his lap. He ignored my anger completely and kept rubbing my scalp, nails teasing my skin every now and then until my eyes got heavy. The next thing I knew, I was out.

Being a girl from Upstate New York, I wasn't a stranger to the cold. But the moment we stepped off the private plane a cold I can only describe as sharp and wet slapped me so hard in the face. I almost regretted coming.

"Shit, I forgot how cold Berlin can feel," Saysha said as she zipped passed me towards the entrance of the private airport we landed in.

Deidre shook her head at her but followed behind her swiftly. Everyone also went towards the entrance while I lagged behind. My mind was racing a million miles a minute.

I prayed that they were okay and knew that Mommy was doing whatever to get them back. Even if it went against their father's wishes to accompany saving them.

The men had spoken to each other about the plan, conveniently leaving us women out. I didn't know what they thought was going to happen by not telling us. If the outcome was that we wouldn't sit pretty while they went out being super savers, they had another thing coming.

I might not have been as skilled as Saysha and Deidre, hell, even my sister. But I wasn't useless. I was showing up for our kids, and the moment I laid my eyes on them and ensured they were safe, I was going to slit Javier from ear to ear with a fucking smile on my face.

And if Carter's mom knew any better, then she better not have anything to do with them being taken, or I was going to do her in next.

Do her in next? I laughed at my unhinged thoughts.

This was the very reason I chose not to get into the family line of work within the Sivad. It never sat right with me how cavalier people were with the lives of others. How it was so easy to manipulate people's lives to fit where it would benefit you.

Don't get me wrong, Sivad was basically white collar when it came to the criminal underworld, but that didn't mean they didn't get dirty.

My mother had trained me and Solelei well before we hit puberty how to use a person's own mind to shape reality to benefit our needs.

It was always a struggle for me to do that, but Solelei took to it like a fish in water. They also ensured that we could protect ourselves and would often have us train with the Davis sisters to sharpen our skills.

I knew Solelei still kept up with it, but other than kickboxing, gun range visits, and sporadic Krav Maga classes, I was most likely the weakest person here.

Stepping into what seemed to be a luxury lounge, I didn't even have to look up to know that Carter and Gerasimou were watching me.

I chose to ignore them and go to where the women were sitting next to each other talking. Silently, I sat down next to my sister laying my head on her right shoulder. Without faltering her conversation, Solelei nestled my cheek with her right hand, pressing me gently into her.

For a few seconds, I let myself exist there, pressed into my sister's warmth, letting her heartbeat slow the chaos in my head. This was something we used to do to each other whenever we felt out of sorts and in need of grounding. I closed my eyes allowing the slow beat of her heart to relax me. The lounge around us was quiet except for the muted shuffle of people settling in. The men spoke in low tones on the other side of the room, Carter and Gerasimou's voices calling to me even though I didn't want to answer.

I could still feel it without looking. Both of them stared at me, waiting for what? I didn't know nor care at the moment. I refused to give either of them the satisfaction.

Solelei's thumb stroked the side of my face. "Breathe," she murmured. "Let your mind settle."

I tried, but my chest still felt tight. Everything in me was wired, stretched thin like a live wire ready to snap. My hands curled into fists in my lap before I forced them to relax.

I felt crazy. One moment, I felt fine and hopeful. The next, I felt like my heart was being ripped from my body, only to moments later, to be fuming mad. Or so fucking needy for the two men who basically abandoned me.

"Chelle called me," my sister said randomly.

"Shit." Opening my eyes, I muttered a curse under my breath.

With everything going on since the twins were taken, I hadn't even thought about the fact my best friend Chelle would be losing her shit not hearing from me.

"It's okay. I let her know that there was shit going on, and you broke your phone," Solelei stated.

"She is probably still flipping out. Especially not being able to have access to the twins." I adjusted myself on her shoulder. "Did you tell her what was going on?"

"No, I did not," she answered. "Although you aren't actively a part of the Sivad, you are still under its protection. Which means the grace is extended to the twins. Them being taken is Sivad business. You know we cannot share without clearance."

She was right. If there was one thing drilled into us, it was that we did not share Sivad business. So much so that my family's job was to rectify and break individuals mentally who thought they could defy the rules.

"I know, I know." I rubbed my eyes, exhausted. "Once I get the twins back, I'll call her and tell her something."

Solelei hummed her agreement then jumped back into conversation with Deidre and Saysha. I sat quietly listening but not engaging. They were mostly talking about mundane things, and truly, I didn't have the mental capacity to fake like I cared.

"Aye, lads and lasses," Fin called out. I sat up and saw him coming from behind a door with a tablet in his hand. Without looking up, he simultaneously typed as he walked. "I just spoke to Ayela, and she informed—"

"I'm sorry, who?" Saysha asked, standing abruptly.

"Red," Ivor called to her.

She whipped her to him, and they quietly argued without words before she continued. "Ayela who, Fin? 'Cause I know ya not talkin' 'bout that posh bitch I tagged with Fay when she tried her."

Fin finally pulled his eyes from his device for the first time, giving Saysha his attention. His face was blank almost like he was bored by her outburst. I looked around and short from Smalls and the guys he came with, all sported the same look as Fin. Like they were used to her antics.

"As I was saying. I spoke to Ayela, and she said while it was confirmed Javier is not staying at the Citadel, he did put in a request to host an auction there and transfer of sale." He continued like Saysha hadn't said a thing. "Currently, she is blacking out cameras from the main hub within the hotel so we may enter unchecked. She blocked off the entire top floor for us. Give me a few minutes to access the city's surveillance systems to ensure our time here wasn't tracked."

I stood at the same time he dropped his head back into his tablet, walking away without another word. I watched him as he disappeared through the door he came in from.

"The cameras," Deidre said randomly.

"Huh?" I asked, turning to her.

"He uses the cameras that he pulls up on his tablet. That way he doesn't have to waste his time paying attention to where he walks and can focus on the million or so tasks he has daily," she informed me.

I just stared blinking at her because I didn't even realize that I was indeed asking myself how he was able to walk and use the tablet at the same time. An ability I had only ever experienced with her mother, Charisse.

"So, here's what's up." Banks started pulling everyone's attention. "We will be leaving here in separate cars once my man Fin gives us the clear, since there is so many of us. He's gonna give us that blanket to move free to the hotel. But we ain't neva been caught slippin', and we won't now, so we need to take different routes there.

"Saints, y'all gonna split between the four cars. Lorelei, you're with ya shadows. Deidre and Fin, y'all in one car. Ivor, you and crazy together." Saysha flicked him off, and we all laughed. "Baby, you with me. "

Banks directed that to Solelei, and she blushed. My sister, the cynical hard ass, blushed. *And baby?* Like she knew I was shocked, she gave me a look that screamed to not pry. However, if I had something to focus my mind on instead of the unknown of today's events, I was definitely going to pry.

"If y'all ain't got shit else to add, then sit tight until it's time." He nodded and left in through the same door Fin had.

"Lo, don't start." Solelei glared at me.

"Start what? I just wanted to know how long *that* has been going on," I mused. "Last I checked, you was as single as a dollar bill."

"I am still very much single, Lorelei," she said exasperatedly.

"The way that man called you baby and gave you that look before leaving this lounge says differently."

"Well, I say, Lo. I say," she snapped, then sighed, rubbing her forehead. "It's complicated, and right now I do not want to waste my mental energy on him when I need to use it to get our babies back."

I saw the look in her eyes that felt all too familiar. Instead of pushing her further, I pulled her into a hug tightly. The hug only lasted moments before Banks was back.

"Aight, everyone, let's roll."

And we did. Like a well-oiled machine, we filed into our assigned cars headed to the hotels to finally get my babies back.

Carter

Once we were settled in the hotel, it felt like the signal for war sounded. The entire top penthouse of the Citadel shifted in seconds, we converted the entire living room into our command center without anyone having to say a word.

On the massive mounted flatscreen, Fin already had the new countdown to the auction pulled up. Bright, unforgiving digits ticked away our time.

Less than twenty-one hours.

Everyone gathered in, as we started locking in the final pieces of the plan.

"Nah, man, I don't think that's gonna work." Banks argued at the plan to let Solelei be the buyer.

"What ya mean, '*nah man.*' That's perfect. No one knows who she is outside of us," Saysha argued back.

"No, Banks is right," Solelei agreed with him.

"Of course, you'll say that, cher," Saysha teased.

Solelei blushed, and truly, I was surprised she could show any emotion other than contempt for me.

"No, they're right. Having her go in as the buyer is risky. What if Javier is the one doing the hand off? She and Lorelei favor each other, and he knows her, Deidre pointed out.

"Damn," Saysha conceded. "I never realized that, but you do look a lot alike. Solelei is just darker."

"So, if we can't do it that way, what do we do then?" Lorelei asked no one in particular.

I could feel her leg bounce as she sat between me and G, with nervous energy. Placing my hand on it, I gave her a reassuring squeeze, and G took her hand, giving her the same effect.

"We need someone who they wouldn't expect to be there," I added.

Everyone started giving their ideas all at once. Talking over one another. None of it helpful or making sense. We didn't have time to argue over what to do. We needed a solid plan.

"I can do it," Kilt spoke up.

Peace looked over to Kilt. "You sure, brother?"

We waited for his answer. The ones of us who knew him were surprised at his offering, because Kilter wasn't the kind of man who made himself known. He was more of the dark presence lingering in the shadow.

Riker, before Kilter could answer, nodded his head, agreeing. "That can work. I mean, his antisocial ass stays out of the way enough that they wouldn't know him."

"You cool with that?" Kilt asked both G and I.

"If you down for it, we good, brother," G answered, catching Kilt's forearm and sliding into their Saints' grip, knuckles tapping before the quick chest tap that sealed it.

"Fin, was there any word on the currency of payment?" I asked.

He didn't answer right away. Normally, it wouldn't bother me, but time was of the essence, and we were down to its final wire. "Finlay!" Deidre snapped.

"Ack, sorry, lass." He looked up briefly before looking back down. "I heard ya about the money. Ayela—"

"Fucking bitch," Saysha mumbled.

"Red!" Ivor corrected her, and she rolled her eyes.

"Saysha, Ah knae ya have an issue with the lass, but she has been monumental in helping get the lass' wee babies back." He pinned Saysha with a look.

"Nobody is checking for that girl. She already proved she can't beat my ass." Saysha flicked her wrist like the whole topic bored her. "Anyway. Go on."

Fin shot her a look, clearly wanting to respond, but thought better of it and kept talking. Good choice.

"The payment for the sale," he continued, "is done digitally through private IPs the Nash's issue themselves. My plan is to send the payment, but it won't actually be real."

Yume frowned. "Not real how?"

"The Sivad keeps dummy accounts for situations like this," Deidre answered before Fin could. "They show a balance, but there's nothing actually there."

"So, it's like crypto?" Yume pressed.

"No, lass, not quite." Fin pulled up a blank document on the screen. "Look here. The money is basically a ghost. Looks legitimate. Has no substance."

He started sketching out the process, demonstrating how the shell account would appear to transfer funds. I didn't care about any of it. I would have handed over every cent I owned if it meant getting my kids back.

"If money is the problem, I'll pay it," Lorelei said firmly. "I don't care what it costs. I just want my babies."

"It's not the money, lass," Fin reassured her. "Truth be told, the minimum bid for this auction is pocket change for us."

A low murmur of agreement passed through the room.

We spent another hour tightening the last screws on the plan until there was nothing left to adjust. Every role assigned. Every route mapped. Every risk analyzed.

If everything held... if no one slipped... this would end clean.

Our kids would be safely in the arms of their mother well before Christmas.

And Javier would be met with the barrel of my gun for his transgressions.

"Carter, can I speak with you?" Deidre approached me in the kitchen as I grabbed a bottle of water.

I nodded, taking a sip, as I waited for her to inform me of what I knew was going to challenge me.

"After Kilter has the twins safely in his possession, I know you have plans on eliminating Javier Giraldo." She held my eye contact.

If she was expecting me to respond, I wasn't. There was no reason, because as she stated, she knew what I was going to do, just as much as I knew what she was going to say next.

"We need him brought in alive." My stomach flipped, but I didn't allow it to show on my face.

The thought of letting him live did not anger me. It simply made no sense. There was no universe where his life extended beyond the moment my children were safe.

"Deidre." I warned.

"It is understood, and I am not saying you cannot be the one to kill him. However, there is something bigger at play, and we need to question him," she explained, reaching on the counter for her own water. "The Sivad needs intel he has."

Her displaying that it was the Sivad calling for Javier to live only made me want to tell her that I was not a member of the Sivad, and the rules of compliance did not extend to me.

However, I knew with my affiliation to the Brorskap and my loyalty to Henrik, I would grant them this. Barely.

But I had my own terms.

Before I voiced them, I let my eyes shift past her. Lorelei sat stiffly next to G, listening to Fin break down the plan yet again. She didn't know I was watching her, didn't feel the way my focus locked on her like a blade sinking home. Her shoulders were tight with worry, her face drawn. She kept gnawing at her bottom lip like she was holding on to the last thread of sanity she had left.

That was all it took.

A quiet vow carved itself in place inside me. Not rage. Not heat. Just truth. Cold. Final.

Javier Giraldo would not leave Berlin breathing once my children were back in her arms.

Questions or not.

Useful or not.

He was already dead.

He just hadn't realized he was walking toward the end I had prepared for him.

I brought my attention back to Deidre.

"I will bring him in alive," I said calmly. "You have my word on that."

Her eyes narrowed slightly, not in suspicion, but in acknowledgment that she heard what I did not say.

Alive was temporary.

Alive was a condition.

Alive was not a promise of survival.

And the moment he served his use... that condition would be revoked.

Lorelei

Snow drifted past the floor-to-ceiling windows in slow, lazy spirals—soft, delicate, completely at odds with the rot sitting in my stomach.

From the penthouse height, the city below looked like a living Christmas postcard. People bundled in winter coats rushed between glowing storefronts, bags bumping against their legs as they tried to make someone's holiday perfect. A family paused in front of the giant tree in the plaza, the father lifting his daughter onto his shoulders so she could touch the lowest ornament.

For a moment, I let myself imagine the story behind each person down there. A mother hunting for the last toy her son asked Santa for. A couple grabbing matching pajamas because it was their first Christmas living together. Someone hurrying home with peppermint hot chocolate with the people they loved fueling them.

All that warmth. All that joy.

I should've been in that spirit too. I should be at home with my babies. We should've been knee deep in gingerbread houses, sugar cookies, and deciding whether or not their hot cocoa needed more cinnamon.

Woflie would scrunch his cute face and tell me '*no simanem, Mama*', and I would correct him to say cinnamon. Dreamie would be her quiet, silent self, happy to have her treat.

I should be exhaustedly finding new shit for their twin elves on the shelf to do. Keeping the sparkle of Christmas magic.

I should have my fucking babies.

That feeling of my chest tightening started, air began to feel like a distant concept. Before I had a moment to succumb to the panic I was being pulled under, I felt strong arms wrap around me.

Gerasimou lifted me into a bridal hold walking us to the couch where he held me in his lap. Without the need to think about it too much, I gripped the front of his signature black t-shirt in my hands, using it and his scent to ground me.

The moisture from his shirt let me know I was crying. While I should have been embarrassed, I wasn't. I knew I needed to be strong, but I just didn't know how to be.

One would think being this close to having them back would be enough to kill the doubt. In fact, it did the exact opposite for me. All I could think about was every possible thing that could go wrong. The danger my babies were in.

But even plagued by everything, the moment Gerasimou lifted me, they started to lessen. And when Carter joined us on that couch, it was almost like putting on noise cancelling headphones. With one, I felt the pain less, but with them both near, it was almost nonexistent.

"You're exhausted, baby," Gerasimou stated rather than asked, like he knew me so innately. He spoke low and deep, the sound settling in my chest.

Every time I heard him call me baby, *lykáki*, or any term of endearment in that low, dark voice with a tinge of his Greek accent, it did something to me. Shit, when they both did it, it was euphoric.

"You barely slept," Carter chimed in.

They were right. I barely slept last night in anticipation for today. I turned to the large flat screen on the wall that displayed the countdown to the auction. We had less than three hours left before Fin submitted our first bid.

I was putting the fate of my children in the hands of people I didn't know. But they had proven to me in six days' time that I could.

Maybe the Sivad wasn't as bad as I felt it was.

"Sleep, *Lykáki*," Gerasimou ordered.

And like my body and mind were waiting on his command and Carter's massaging of my legs, I closed my eyes, drifting into a deep sleep.

Something snatched me from my sleep. Almost like when you have a nightmare and your body forces yourself to wake up. The thing was, I wasn't sure if I was dreaming in order for that to happen. When I opened my eyes, I was disoriented and confused about where I was or how long I had been out. The room was mostly empty with the exception of Fin which eased the slight panic that started to settle in my chest. Flashing light from the flat screen had me sitting up so quickly, I made myself dizzy.

Four minutes and thirty-three seconds.

I blinked.

Four minutes and thirty seconds.

I blinked again.

And it seemed the time either jumped, or I was in the process of having a fucking stroke. Before I could conclude which was happening, the alarm sounded off loudly. Or to me, it felt loud.

Like a category five hurricane warning alarm.

Fin didn't look my way, just continued to tap feverishly on his tablet, when he said, "It's time."

The way he said it—flat, steady—hit me harder than the alarm itself.

This wasn't a drill.

It was time to put in our auction bid.

Everything snapped into motion.

This was the moment we got our twins back.

Or we'd died trying.

"Kilt and Peace will meet you and Solelei here, *Yume*," Carter explained like we hadn't gone over the plan a million times.

We were standing behind a large pillar about twenty feet from where the meeting room Kilter was to enter in ten minutes. My stomach was flipping, and I was chalking it up to the anticipation, but something in my spirit felt like something was going to go wrong.

I couldn't shake the feeling all day, and now as time grew closer, down to the minutes, that our children were going to be back with us, the feeling worsened standing so damn close.

"Do not leave this area until Kilter and Peace hand you the twins, *Lykáki*." Gerasimou clarified further. "I fucking mean it, Lorelei, stay with your sister and Smalls."

I nodded my head. Him and Carter were supposed to be on the other side of the area on the north entrances. We were on the south end. Ivor and Saysha took the west. Deidre and Fin were in the security room of the hotel watching everything as they relayed it into the comms Banks supplied us with.

Banks and Riker came over with identical long black duffle bags slung over their shoulder, and my sister slightly tensed next to me. Looking at her, she didn't show a sign of being bothered on her face. It was carefully blank, but I knew my sister. She was feeling Banks as much as he was feeling her. Honestly, there was probably more going on with them, but with Solelei, you would never know.

"Everything good?" Carter asked Banks.

"You already know, C," Banks stated nonchalantly. "You know I'm not new to this."

Gerasimou dapped him up, pulling him into a brotherly hug. "We know you're true to this." He confirmed what Banks started to say.

"You see anything outta ordinary..."

"We knock that shit back to normal."

It was Carter's turn to dap him up the same way and then they each did with Riker and Smalls. They both came to me, placing soft kisses to my lips with lingering stares that spoke more volumes than not, before they left to their posts.

Banks walked up to my sister as Smalls and Riker moved to the side to speak. Unable to look away, I watched as he spoke to her in low whispers, and Solelei nodded while holding her bottom lip between her teeth. Banks kissed her forehead, left cheek, and her right then used his thumb to remove her bottom lip before kissing her.

My sister, the one who claimed to be single, returned his kiss, deepening it. I turned to give them privacy but filed away that after we touched down in Ithaca, I would be getting the real tea on them.

Once he left, I looked down at the synchronized watches we all wore. In less than three minutes, Kilter should have gotten my babies and been on his way to me. It was going to work. We went over every scenario, and I had to trust the training everyone had. I had to trust that they knew what they were doing.

"Here." My sister held her arm out to me. When I looked down, I realized she had a Smith and Wesson, my favorite brand of guns in her hand. "Take this. I know those fuckers didn't give you anything, but I know what my sister is capable of. *You* know what you are capable of.

"I know they are also capable, and we have meticulously gone over every part of this, but in case not. You get your fucking babies back, Lorelei. Do you hear me?"

I took the gun, checking the clip and the chamber. Other than at a range it had been years since I'd held one in my hand, but it felt familiar and normal. Taking a deep breath, I nodded my head and got into the zone.

The watch beeped. It was time.

"We got eyes on Javier. He has three men with him alone. Ayela is escorting them to the event space." Fin's voice came over the comm giving us play by play.

"I got eyes up top." Banks' smooth ass deep voice came in next. "Dead man comin' through the east."

"I got eyes on Kilt and Peace. They are entering through the south entrance," Riker added.

"Do you think with only two of them, Peace and Kilt are okay when there is four of them?" I asked out loud to anyone who would answer.

"Don't worry, little one. Kilt and Peace are beasts at this kind of shit," Smalls reassured me. "They are going to get our niece and nephew out of there, then your men will put a bullet through his cranium."

I smiled at his light heartedness in such a tense situation. During the short time that I had been around him, I could see so many of Gerasimou's mannerisms in him. During the flight in, Smalls let me in on a bit of Gerasimou's time with them in his late teens and early twenties.

You could hear the brotherly love in his voice, and I was happy that he had them, and by extension, our babies did as well. Just almost a week ago, it was just us and the small family that consisted of my parents, sister, and Chelle and her family. When my babies were back home, they were going to learn they had so many people ready to ignite the solar system to ensure they were always safe.

"Fuck!" Riker whispered angrily.

"What?" we all asked simultaneously.

"Gritt is here, man," he said. I was confused who Gritt was.

"Shit! Do you think he recognized him?" Smalls asked him.

"It doesn't look like it."

I didn't know who they were talking about, but I hoped he didn't recognize Kilter and this whole thing exploded.

"*Senor* Elias Knox!" Javier's heavy Latin accent made my skin crawl. I was surprised to hear him on the comm. "Thank you so much, my friend, for your purchase. I almost don't want to give them up because they are such a sweet prize."

The way he spoke of my children had me coaching myself to stay put and not shoot him in his dick.

"No, thank you," Kilter answered smoothly. "Did you have any issues acquiring your payment?" he asked him.

"Not at all, mi amigo. The 8.7 million has been accepted." I could almost hear the slimy smile in his voice. This man was nothing like the Jason who befriended me at Ithaca Grace. "I hope in the future we can do business again. While I am unsure if it would be as rare as this one."

"Speaking of my purchase..." Kilter dragged.

"Oh, yes, we wanted to make sure you were clean before we gave them to you. Since they are young, I will throw in their nanny," Javier explained. I heard someone speaking hushly, but it was too low for me to make out what he said. "While they are in prime and perfect condition, they can be little hellions. The nanny made herself useful since they are comfortable with her."

Kilter responded, and they continued a conversation so naturally, I had to remind myself that Kilter wasn't a bad man and really bought my kids to do God knows what with.

After a few minutes, Fin broke through the comm. "Ayela's assistant is en route to the meeting location in t-two minutes."

My heart began to speed up. At first I didn't understand if Ayela had access to my babies, why couldn't she just grab them and hand them to us? Deidre explained that the Nash's were a neutral family. Meaning they aided everyone in the criminal underworld. As heiress to *The Keepers*, it was imperative that she kept her neutrality because the discourse that would come from word getting out that she assisted us would be monumental and call for the dismantlement of the *Keepers*.

I remembered learning briefly from my mother who the *Keepers* were and their importance to all of us.

"I got eyes on the wee babes," Fin stated.

"I have eyes." Riker came in next.

"Smalls." Carter's voice came in clipped.

"On it."

I fought to get free, but just because his name was Smalls didn't mean he was a small man. There was no way I could free myself.

"Ah, there they are! Perfect, aye?" he asked, laughing and clapping his hands. "And look at this young piece of ass. If you choose to wait to sample or do whatever you will with the children, I can promise you the nanny here will make up for it."

I almost threw up hearing him admit to raping Celeste. My heart broke for her, and guilt turned my stomach more. Solelei put her hand on my shoulder, and I already knew she was thinking the same thing I was. Solelei would help her through this once she was ready to open up about it.

From the sound of it, everything was going well until it didn't. I heard a man curse loudly and say it was a set up. The sounds of my babies screaming and guns shooting caused everything around me to freeze. In a split second, I made my decision.

Solelei must have noticed it too. "Lo..." she warned, but my mind was made up.

Lifting my body that was still being held by Smalls, I kicked Solelei back, causing her to fall into one of the accent chairs to the ground. Next, I bit down, hard, on Smalls' hand until I tasted copper.

In a sharp hiss, he loosened his hold enough for me to break free and run straight to the door. A chorus of voices flooded my comm, all telling me to stop, but I couldn't.

No, fuck that, I wouldn't.

G

I'd been on many contracts since I joined the *Brorskap* with Carter. Before joining, I was an active member of a ruthless MC where I was no stranger to violence or to action. None of it moved me. None of it struck fear in my heart.

However, the fucking moment I heard the sounds of guns being let off and Solelei say *Lykáki's* name in a warning, I knew exactly what she was going to do. And for the first time in my fucked-up existence, real fear settled in my chest.

I looked over to Carter. On the same line of thinking, we took off for the entrance where we were stationed. The entire plan we meticulously went over was thrown out the window.

We entered the same time *Lykáki* did, she immediately ducked low in the protection of its alcove as bullets whizzed in her direction, landing outside the door she entered. A man was advancing towards her with her not noticing him as she shielded herself from the onslaught of bullets.

"*Yume*!"

"*Lykáki*!"

Carter and I boomed over the cacophony of violence shredding the air. She lifted her head the same time I lifted my gun to shoot, but he dropped when a throwing star caught his carotid artery.

Riker or Peace hadn't alerted us there was anyone in the room besides them, Javier, his men, and Ayela's assistant with the twins. I assumed to keep their cover. However, based on that scary son of a bitch's numbers compared to ours, he clearly had men waiting inside in case anything popped off.

Shit was absolute chaos.

I spotted Kilter and Peace ducked behind a table they flipped over, giving the fuckers a run for their money. My brothers could hold their own on any given day, and being against about ten or twelve of Javier's guys was no different.

"I want Mama!" Dream cried loud enough for us to hear over the noise, and Loralei's head snapped in her direction.

Everything snapped in one violent shift.

She didn't slow down to register or assess what was happening. From my view, I saw how she took in Dream in Javier's arms, Wolfe struggling in another man's grip in a nanosecond, and her whole body locked onto them like a loaded arrow.

Then she moved.

Not with rage. Not with panic.

With purpose. Sharp and lethal.

She cut through the center of the room at a speed I didn't know she possessed. One of Javier's men stepped into her path. She dropped low and slid across the floor, gun drawn, firing two shots in each of his calves before he ever fully turned. He hit the ground screaming, and she was already past him.

Carter stayed tight on my right as we pushed through the floor, picking off any threat trying to angle toward Loralei. Not that anyone was keeping up with her.

She was a blur.

Another man lunged—she vaulted over his back, twisted, and drove her knee into the next one's jaw mid-landing. He dropped instantly.

Seeing her be so ruthless to get to our children filled my chest with pride. Javier stumbled backward, dragging Dream with him, eyes flicking between escape routes that were disappearing by the second. The panic was finally hitting him as he watched his men diminish, slowly leaving him unprotected. One of his stand men dragged Wolfe as he fought to get free.

Not an ounce of fear in his little body almost like he was zoned in to help himself, his sister.

The man made the wrong move grabbing Wolfe by his hair. His pained cries filled every vein in my body with liquid fire. Aiming my gun at him, *Lykáki* knew my next move as if I spoke it to her. She yelled to Wolfe. "Wolfie, close your eyes!" Both Wolfe and Dream looked in her direction, and without question, they closed their eyes.

One shot between the man's eyes dropped him.

Instead of running toward his mother, Wolfe went to where Javier held Dream as if she was a human shield.

Javier had a sinister smile on his face as he also grabbed Wolfe despite him fighting his hold.

"Javier!" Carter barked, but the man only tightened his grip, dragging Wolfe closer as if using him the same. We all froze, unsure what move to make without putting the twins in jeopardy.

I knew me and Carter both, and anyone here were excellent shots, but that didn't mean Javier would move just enough that our shot wouldn't be in the direct path of one of our children.

"Turtle Shell!" Solelei's voice suddenly cut through the chaos.

The twins snapped into it instantly. Not a second wasted.

Dream went first. Her tiny teeth clamped down hard on Javier's forearm, biting with all the frustration and terror packed into her three-year-old body. She screamed, then curled forward, tucking her chin to her chest, and dropped her weight like a rock. Her arms wrapped around herself, a perfect little protective shell, forcing Javier to adjust his hold or risk dropping her.

Wolfe followed once he noticed Javier was distracted, trying to hold his sister. He threw his head up sharply, a practiced flick to snap Javier's jaw shut, then dropped his weight down as well. The movement yanked Javier off balance just enough that his grip loosened on both of them, landing the twins to the ground.

"Moon!" Solelei called out again as she snapped the neck of a man in her path. The command put the twins into action as they locked hands and found a place to hide.

Javier stumbled, trying to regain control. His sinister smile faltered, but barely, as he realized the children were no longer in his possession.

That fraction of a second was all Loralei needed. She surged forward, sliding under one of Javier's men who lunged at her, and landed a perfectly timed strike that forced him backward. Something in me knew she needed to be the one to finish this. Carter might not agree, but together, we moved immediately into the opening, clearing space for her.

Loralei was on Javier in a heartbeat, taking advantage of his lack of balance. She drop-kicked his ass to the ground while the rest of us took out his men, leaving just him for my *Lykáki*.

Carter

I died a thousand deaths watching *Yume* make her way through the mirage of violence. Many times I wanted to rush to her and pull her away. But as I watched in a mixture of awe and pride, I knew then what her sister meant in the room on the plane.

She was a force.

Maybe the fantasy I built over the last four years made me judge her wrong, thinking she needed us to save our children and protect her, and that we'd have to babysit her the whole way.

Yume studied Javier like a lioness did her prey while he stood there with blood trickling down his lip–the aftermath of my son uppercutting him with his head.

When Solelei called those commands and the twins reached for them, I wasn't surprised in the least. It's what I would have done if I had known about them.

"Ayela has the wee babes," Fin announced on the comm.

That was all *Yume* needed. Before any of us could register it, she delivered a powerful kick to Javier's face, sending him and some of his teeth to the ground.

Javier turned on his back, blood covering his teeth as he laughed. He *laughed*, mocking the pain he had caused.

The fear.

Loralei snapped, leaping on him, and began to beat him in the face with a gun I still wasn't sure how she got. The entire time she beat him in the face, he laughed.

Standing abruptly, she began kicking him before she aimed the gun, now dripping with his blood, at him, her chest rising and falling rapidly. Whether it was because she was out of breath from beating him senseless or because she was battling taking his life or not was something I couldn't tell.

"Carter! Do not let her kill him." Deidre's voice came through my comm. A quick glance around let me know we were on a private line. "We need him alive."

I closed my eyes, battling with my own decision. On one hand, he deserved the permanent solution of death. On the other, we had been fighting human trafficking rising in the Sivad, and he might have answers we'd been attempting to retrieve for the last four years.

The click of Loralei putting a bullet into the chamber forced me to decide. Walking up to her leisurely, I placed a hand on her forearm. Her head whipped to me. Since she faced away from most of us, we couldn't see her face. Tears streamed down her face, but I could tell that it wasn't from sadness.

It was anger.

White hot anger burned brightly in her eyes.

Even with her facing me, she still held her gun trained on him.

"Drop the gun, *Yume-chan*," I said calmly.

Her eyes narrowed on me. "Drop the gun?" she asked incredulously.

"Yes, I know how much you want to kill him, but we cannot."

"I know you're fucking lying?!" Saysha hissed. "Do not listen to him, Lo, kill his ass."

"Red!" Ivor barked.

"I'm real sick of you tryna always hush me with ya big ass." Saysha turned her ire towards Ivor. They stood in a staring match with each other.

I found myself breathing in deep yet again, this time attempting to calm myself from lashing out on them. This wasn't the time or place. Her outburst caused a few to also voice that the only choice was to end Javier's miserable life. I was partial to the same outcome, but orders were orders, and it wasn't in my learned conditioning to defy when a job was asked of me.

"Look at me, *Yume*," I said loud enough for only her to hear me.

She looked from me to our small group, her hand tightening on the 9mm. She looked down to a now groaning Javier then back to me then to G. He stood there stoic. I hadn't told him what Deidre asked of me. I knew he wasn't in the favor of keeping him alive from the beginning more so now after the way he handled our children.

Kuso! Betrayal was evident in both of their eyes–a look I'd seen before but never from Dimitri and not one I wanted to see from *her*. I didn't want them to think I was choosing this waste of life.

"Why?" she asked barely above a whisper.

"We have to," I answered simply, even though the reasoning was deeper than that.

"Have to?!" she scoffed. "You're right, we have to end his sorry fucking existence."

"I know, and he will pay for his transgression, b—"

"His transgressions?!" she roared. "He stole my kids! Our kids. And you're asking me to spare his life?"

"I am asking you to trust me!" I roared.

She jumped, eyes wide. She dropped the gun to her side as she looked at me bewildered until it morphed into recognition then anger.

"Trust you? Because he is your brother? Is that why?"

Before I could answer, the door opened near us, and we all aimed our weapons to it. Deidre walked through with a blank expression like eleven people didn't have a copious amount of firearms pointed at her. "No, because the Sivad ordered it," she stated calmly like the room wasn't dripping in carnage. "I know it is asking a lot for you to let us take him in alive. But he had top involvement with the human trafficking that has been seeping into our organization. If we kill him now, more mothers will be put in the same position you were in.

"I'm requesting this from you, Loralei. But it's an order, nonetheless. Do this, and I promise you that everyone involved will pay for causing you and the twins pain."

Yume gnawed at her bottom lip, nostrils flaring, cheeks red. Her eyes blinked feverishly before she conceded, dropping her arm yet again.

"Thank you, Loralei. I kn—" Deidre's words were cut off by two consecutive shots ringing out.

Javier began screaming as much as he could with a dislocated jaw. She did it so swiftly, I missed the action of her raising her arm again.

Turning, *Yume* began walking, calling over her shoulder. "You don't need your legs to be alive."

We all stood there, some in awe, some in surprise. But the women wore a look of pride seeing her stand in her power.

"Fin," I heard her in my comm. "Bring me my kids," she ordered before disappearing through the door.

Loralei

I made it to the penthouse in a daze. I could only imagine what I looked like walking through the hotel to the elevators. There wasn't a way that blood didn't cover my body from the amount of men I dropped and the beating I gave that motherfucker.

No matter how much training I had as a child, no matter how many times I went to the gun range, or how much I'd seen working in a trauma hospital in Aurora. None of that prepared me to take a life. I swore under oath as a medical professional to do no harm, and I dropped more bodies in that event space than I cared to count.

The thing that rattled me wasn't the fact that I killed those men or that I beat Javier to an inch of his life. No. What I had a difficult time coming to terms with was that it was so easy. That holding that 9mm in my hand felt like it was an extension of me. Shooting it felt like breathing.

And killing them felt like home.

I never wanted to be the kind of person who could take a life without feeling it.

Today... I was.

Truth was, I would do that shit again in a fucking heartbeat, if it meant my kids would be safe. I would be the villain, the harborer of death. I would eradicate entire blood lines behind Wolfe and Dream Kincaid.

Turning the shower head on, I quickly removed my clothes soiled with blood and stepped in. The water already scorching and exactly what I needed to shed this layer of myself. Quickly, I scrubbed myself in anticipation for Fin to bring me my babies. I couldn't see them after damn near a week in this rage when I should feel joy being reunited with them. To be able to kiss them, hug them. Hear their little voices calling my name.

I didn't. I felt rage.

The need to end Javier, no, every scum of the earth tied to him, pressed at the forefront of my psyche. It was so tangible I could taste it.

The sound of the bathroom door opening caused me to pause like it was an intruder, knowing I knew who it was. I could feel him.

"*Lykáki*." Gerasimou calling out that name would forever make my heart skip several beats. His voice was soft. Too soft for him.

I didn't say anything. Eyes closed, back to him, I continued my task of scrubbing my body. I didn't want to have a conversation. All I wanted was to cleanse myself of this feeling and to be with my babies. That was it, that was all.

He was now standing at the entrance of the doorless shower. I could feel his eyes on me. Waiting... wanting me to acknowledge him. As much as I didn't want to, I knew if I didn't, he would just stand there silently until I did. Sighing heavily, I turned to face him.

The moment our eyes met, something inside me flinched. He wasn't looking at me like he usually did—hungry, sure of himself, ready to take the world apart if it meant having me close.

No.

This was different.

It was gentler.

And that softness on him felt wrong, unfamiliar, like seeing a weapon bent the wrong way.

I didn't want gentle.

Not now.

Not with the rage still simmering under my skin, still coating my tongue like metal.

"*Lykáki*..." he said again, quieter this time.

I hated the way it made my chest twist.

"I'm fine, Dimitri," I muttered, turning away, scrubbing harder at my skin like I could peel the day off layer by layer.

He didn't argue.

That alone made my pulse jump. Gerasimou was one to call me out. He met my bullshit head-on, knocked it out of my hand before I could finish spinning whatever narrative I spun.

But now?

Silence.

A heavy one.

One that filled the whole damn bathroom.

The next thing I heard was the sound of fabric hitting water.

I jerked around, eyes flying open just in time to see him step fully dressed under the shower with me. Boots, tactical pants, shirt—soaked instantly. He didn't flinch. Didn't blink. Water poured over him like he'd walked into a battlefield, not a bathroom. The black fabric sticking to him like a second skin, defining every hard plane on his body.

"Gerasimou—" I started, but he cut me off by just being there. Close. Too close.

His hand lifted slowly, like he was giving me every second to pull back; even though he'd never needed permission from me before. His fingers brushed my arm, feather-light.

Too light.

"Don't do that," I whispered, voice cracking in a way I despised.

He stilled.

"Do what?" he asked, tone almost careful.

"Be... this." I gestured at him, soaked, gentle, eyes full of a quiet I didn't know how to handle at the moment. "I can't... I don't want that."

His jaw flexed, and something sharp flashed in his gaze. The part of him I knew. The man made of steel and heat and unyielding devotion.

"It's not softness," he murmured. "It's restraint."

My breath caught.

"And I'm using every bit of it not to pull you into me right now and hold you until you stop shaking. To not do the only fucking thing I can to return you to yourself."

I didn't realize I was shaking until he said it.

I clenched my fists, nails digging into my palms. "I don't need... comfort. I need my children."

"Our children. And you'll have them," he said, stepping closer, so close I could feel the heat from him even with the water. "But you're going to look at me first. Because you're here with me, not out there spilling blood."

His fingers brushed my cheek, the barest touch, and I sucked in a breath.

"I don't want to feel anything right now," I whispered.

He took my hand and pressed it to his chest. The steady thump of his heart matched the rhythm of the water hitting us from the showerhead. I felt it pulse beneath my palm.

"Do you feel that?" he asked.

I could only nod.

Then he took my other hand and brought it to my chest, holding it there.

"And this? Do you feel your heart beating?"

I exhaled shakily. "Dimitri—"

"No," he cut in softly. "Feel it. My heart beats. Your heart beats. That means blood is still moving through us, *Lykáki*. That means we woke up today. And as fucked up as this world is..." He leaned his forehead to mine. "We still get to live and breathe another day."

We stayed like that for... I don't even know how long. Time didn't exist between his heartbeat and mine.

Then the sweetest sound broke through the steam—tiny giggles drifting from the other side of the door. Our tether snapped back into place.

"And that," he murmured, nodding toward the closed bathroom door, "to preserve that... to protect that? We will wipe the life of any motherfucker who dares to take it, to harm it, to alter it. Clean off this fucking solar system."

His hand slid to the back of my neck, pulling me closer until his nose brushed mine. His voice dropped to a low, razor-steady growl.

"Do not let what you had to do to protect our children sit heavy in you. Do you understand me?"

My breath stuttered. I managed a shaky yes. I wanted to say more. *God, I wanted to*, but the words scattered every time I reached for them. Before I could even gather them, Gerasimou took my lips with his. For the first time in damn near a week, real warmth flickered back in my chest.

Loralei

Gerasimou slipped out of the bathroom after getting dressed in the closet, one I hadn't even realized was stocked with clothes. Come to think of it, I hadn't seen a single bag when they boarded the plane. Typical. Men like them did not pack; they planned.

I wanted to go straight to the twins, scoop them up, breathe them in. But I needed a moment to gather myself. I needed to be the mother they knew and expected, not this raw and stripped-down version of m e.

What happened in the shower...

That was not the Gerasimou he introduced himself to me as nor was it the G he was with his colleagues. A presence built from steel, heat and danger, that was the version of him people feared.

What I felt in that moment was different. It was gentler. More open. It belonged to a side of him he never let anyone see. A softness that felt like he kept hidden like his first name.

Whatever part of him that was gave me enough steadiness to breathe again.

But the rest was on me. I had to pull myself together. I had to greet our children in a way that reminded them they were safe. They deserved that version of me.

I made a mental note to talk to Solelei or my parents about getting the twins into therapy. They had survived something no child should ever experience. Trauma didn't disappear. It found corners to hide in and waited. I refused to let this settle in their bones without giving them the tools to heal.

There was a light knock at the door. Carter opened it, and we locked eyes.

The softness I expected wasn't there.

What met me instead was frustration he barely could hold onto. It sat in his jaw, in the tight line of his mouth, in the way his shoulders were set. It wasn't rage or cruelty.

I continued to gaze into his beautiful hazel eyes. They were more golden than normal with a glint I'd never seen in them. Almost like *fear*? Was Carter afraid? "Wait, were you afraid?" I asked.

"You ran into an active shootout," he said. Not loud. Not sharp. Flat. Controlled.

I opened my mouth, but he lifted a hand, stopping the words right on my tongue.

"We told you not to come to Berlin," he continued. "Both of us. And you still did." His eyes flicked over me, glossy, taking in the faint bruising from hitting the ground. "Then you ran straight into gunfire."

Fuck! He was truly scared.

"Don't you ever scare us like that." He took my face in his calloused hands.

His words landed heavy and deep in my chest.

"I did what I had to do," I said.

"I know," he replied immediately. Too quickly. "That's the problem. You put yourself in that line of fire. Making yourself susceptible to irreversible harm. Do not make G and I have to look our children in the eyes and tell them we lost their mother. That *we* lost you. Again."

Silence stretched between us, thick with everything said and unsaid.

"They're asking for you," he said, and something in his voice changed. Wonder edged the tension. Awe, barely concealed. "They're... God. They are incredible, *Yume*."

A smile I wouldn't stop even if I could, spread large across my face. Dream and Wolfe were really the best little humans to exist. They had so much of their fathers in them, it was a wonderment.

"You met them?" I asked.

"No. Ayela and Fin brought them to the room, and they've been in the room with Solelei. We felt it would be better to introduce ourselves when you were there."

I let out a breath I hadn't even realized I was holding. It wasn't that I wasn't ready for the twins to know their fathers, I just didn't want it to be without me.

They were so young, they didn't really ask for them, but they knew they had fathers. It was never my intention to keep Gerasimou or Carter from the twins. I just didn't know how to find them.

"I'm angry, Loralei," he admitted. "And I know you are as well. Please know I fought with following this order. But also, I am thankful. And I don't know what to do with both at the same time."

I could have asked him what he meant by that, but I think I knew. Taking Javier's life at that moment would have sent me spiraling more than I already had for the bodies I dropped. Those were for preservation of my life and my babies. Killing his brother would have been personal, for revenge, stimmed by anger, and I wasn't sure I could live with that.

His hand lowered to my wrist, firm and grounding. He lowered his head and kissed my forehead, letting his lips linger long enough to heat my body. Taking my chin in his other hand, he lifted it, so we were locked in each other's stare.

I didn't know what he was searching for in my eyes, but under it, I felt so open and exposed. At the same time, I also felt safe and seen.

These men had the innate ability to spin me in various directions. That should confuse me, or at the very least make me dizzy. Instead, I always felt like they knew exactly where I was headed and would guide me effortlessly.

Closing my eyes seemed like the only way to break the spell he had me under. Only doing so left me unaware of his movements. Warm and soft lips landed on mine in a kiss that settled my spirit.

Just moments ago, Gerasimou kissed me in a way that caused my heart to beat widely trying to connect with his. And here was Carter kissing me, and he made me feel safe in the chaos. Giving me room to be both soft but wild.

The twins' voices came through the closed door as it had when I was in the shower. This time it was clearer, and I allowed their innocence to envelop me while allowing their father to give me a lifeline through his lips.

Breaking apart, I was left breathless and wishing it never ended. Pulling me into his strong chest, I rested there, just for a moment.

"Carter?" I whispered.

"Hmm," he answered, the sound vibrating deep in his chest.

"Would you like to be introduced to your kids?" I lifted my head to look at him.

He blinked rapidly. As I stated before, I never wanted to keep them a part.

With a sharp nod and a barely audible '*hai*', he took my hand and led us to our children.

G

I'd already had my moment with Lykáki. What I needed to say had been said. What she needed from me, I gave. After that, Carter went in to have his time, and I took up position near the bathroom door without a word exchanged between us.

That was how it worked.

One of us stayed close. One of us gave her space. While at the same time making sure the twins were never without one of our eyes on them.

From where I stood, I watched the kids play with Solelei like the day hadn't nearly broken us all. Like they hadn't been taken. Like they hadn't gone almost a week without their mother. They were loud, messy, fully absorbed in whatever world they'd built on the floor. Toy cars, babies, and soft voices scattered everywhere.

They didn't notice me.

Not once did either of them acknowledge my presence. Even as I stood here, a large stranger that to some would seem alarming, they just kept on playing like I didn't exist in their world yet. And that was okay with me. For now. I wanted the first time I was introduced to the twins, it was with Carter and Loralei present.

Solelei noticed me though.

She shot me a look from where she sat with them, sharp and measuring. I kept my face blank, not allowing whatever feelings she had with me to affect me. She might have been *Lykáki's* sister, but whatever her issue was had nothing to do with my kids.

The twins' innocence and resilience were a phenomenon to witness. Something about it stirred parts of me I'd buried under survival and violence a long time ago. I didn't grow up like that. My childhood had been stripped down early by poverty and by people who knew how to spot something soft and ruin it.

Anyone who thought my drive to get those kids back was just about Lykáki didn't understand shit.

It was about what I'd seen. What I'd done. What had been done to me.

If giving my last breath meant those two never had to learn this world the way I did, I'd do it without hesitation.

"Mama!" Dream squealed the moment the bathroom door opened, rushing to her mother.

Wolfe had been on the floor beside Solelei, lining up a handful of toy cars she must've scavenged from somewhere in the penthouse. At the sound of his sister's voice, his head snapped up. He froze mid-movement, one small hand hovering over a red truck like time itself stalled.

His eyes, the same golden hazel as Carter's, locked onto their mother.

For a heartbeat, he only stared, processing. Then his gaze locked on *Lykáki* like nothing else in the room existed. The truck slipped from his fingers and clattered against the floor.

"Mama!" he screeched, launching himself toward her the same way Dream did.

Lykáki dropped to her knees and caught them both, their small bodies crashing into her hard enough that she would have fallen if Carter and I hadn't stepped in behind her without thinking. I felt her shake the moment she wrapped them up, felt the way she clung like she needed to anchor herself to something real.

She was crying.

Not quietly, not delicately. She sobbed into their hair, holding them like the world had already tried to steal them once and she wasn't letting it happen again.

Dream soaked it up, smiling and clinging tighter, completely oblivious to now two strange men standing just behind their mom.

Wolfe didn't though. He allowed his mother to give him kisses, and he embraced it, but his eyes were fixated on us, sliding from me to Carter's, and Carter froze.

His sister must have caught on to her brother because her gaze slipped to ours, and I stilled. Like the air that was moments ago flowing to my lungs was snatched from it.

Seeing her eyes in photographs hadn't prepared me for this.

In person, it was undeniable. The same stormy gray. The same depth that looked like it carried weather in it. The same sharp awareness that clocked a room before she even moved.

Mine.

Dream's gaze locked onto me with a focus that didn't belong to a three-year-old.

"Mama," Wolfe said beside her,too controlled for a child his age.

Lykáki paused, brushing tears from her cheeks. "Yes, baby?"

Dream followed Wolfe's line of sight only for a second before her attention snapped back to me, studying me openly now. Curious. I felt it immediately.

"*¿Quiénes son*?" Wolfe asked.

Carter shifted at my side. Wolfe's use of Spanish caught us both off guard.

Lykáki turned slightly, taking one of their small hands in each of hers. "Well, baby—"

"*Soy tu papa*," Cater blurted, the words leaving me before I had time to sand them down.

Both children frowned the same way *Lykáki* did when something didn't quite line up in her mind.

"He my daddy?" Dream asked.

Lykáki faltered. This wasn't something you rehearsed. How do you explain bloodlines and biology to toddlers when even adults struggled to understand it? Twins with one mother. Two fathers. Hell, I still didn't fully understand it. But their existence was evident love that didn't divide cleanly the way the world demanded it should.

Looking at them, I didn't feel separation.

I felt responsibility.

Carter and I exchanged a brief look.

I lowered myself to their level, resting on the balls of my feet. Yume watched me closely, trusting me to take point. I gave her a look back that told her I would.

"Yes, baby girl," I said evenly. "He..." I nodded toward Carter... "is your papa. As am I."

Dream tilted her head one way, then the other, tapping her chin like she was turning it over carefully. "Hmm..." She glanced at her brother, then back to us. "You's Woflie papa too?"

Carter crouched beside me, smiling wide. "*Sí*. We are also Wolfe's papa."

Dream's face lit up instantly. "Mama! Mama! You hear him? He says him my papas! And him!" She bounced in place like she'd just been handed something precious.

"I hear you," *Lykáki* said softly. "Does that make you happy, Dream girl? What about you, Wolfie?"

Wolfe didn't answer right away. He quietly studied us instead.

Then his eyes went to Carter. "You my papa?"

The resemblance between them was unmistakable up close. Carter didn't blink. "Yeah. Papa."

Wolfe stepped forward, close enough to reach Carter's chest. He pressed his palm there, fingers flexing once, like he was listening for something only he could hear.

Then he turned and did the same to me.

I stayed still, letting him decide.

After a beat, he nodded once. "Okay."

Dream clapped like the verdict had been reached. "See! We gots two papas!"

She launched herself into my arms without hesitation. I laughed, surprised by the sound as I caught her easily. Wolfe stayed where he was, smiling to himself, quiet but sure.

"You like trucks?" he asked Carter.

"I know they're big," Carter answered honestly.

"I got lots," Wolfe said, grabbing his hand. "Come see."

Dream squirmed to be put down. "Papas! Play wit my babies!" She tugged me along behind them like this was already settled business.

Like we weren't trained killers, we followed the direction of toddlers to the floor. Solelei long slipped out the room, leaving this moment for us.

Just us.

Somewhere between rocking an imaginary baby to sleep and orchestrating the most dramatic monster truck crash imaginable, our world narrowed down to five people.

Dream squealed. Wolfe laughed.

I looked up and met Carter's gaze.

Nothing needed to be said.

The five of us were nonnegotiable.

No one was taking that from us.

Not the world.

Not the past.

Not even ourselves.

Carter

"Ahh! Gerasimou stop, before I fall!" Yume's squeals reached me halfway down the stairs.

I'd just gotten the twins down for a much-needed nap, leaving G and her downstairs to finish putting up the rest of the Christmas decorations the twins had refused to let us touch. Apparently, garland was a personal offense if they weren't the ones holding it.

By the time I reached the bottom step, I found Yume perched on G's shoulders, carefully wrapping green garland around the kitchen doorway.

"Woman, just put the damn green thing on the hook," G shot back, his tone all bark and no bite.

His hands were locked around her thighs, firm and protective, like he was daring gravity, fate, or his own intrusive thoughts to try something stupid. She leaned forward to secure the garland, one of her locs slipping loose and brushing his cheek. He huffed when it tickled his face, tightening his grip without even realizing it.

"It's called a garland, Dimitri." She laughed.

"I don't care what the shit's called," He grunted. "Just finish so we can do something else."

Yume playfully slapped his shoulder, and he ran his hand up her thigh squeezing it. A small smile graced my lips in a domestic way that still felt foreign to me. No weapons within reach. No tension threading the air. Just the three of us in a borrowed quiet, pretending the world hadn't tried to tear us apart a week ago.

If I knew this was what it would be like when we left *Yume* alone in that cabin four years ago, there wouldn't be a single way I would have left her. Not to sound like some lovesick imbecile, but since she had come back into our lives two, almost three weeks ago, every reason I existed didn't make sense before.

Just as I knew G felt the same. Regardless of what had brought us together, I'd seen the change in my brother. He wasn't moving through life simply to survive anymore, wasn't measuring time by the space between one violent necessity and the next.

It was one of the few hopes I'd carried for him since we were boys far too young to be shaped by the lives forced onto us. And while I'd been dealt my own version of a fundamentally flawed upbringing, what Dimitri endured had been far more brutal than anything I'd known.

Finally, Yume managed to get the garland exactly where she wanted it. She tapped G lightly on the head, satisfied. "Okay. You can put me down now."

I stepped in without thinking, closing the distance as G reached up from his place on her thighs for her waist. It was unnecessary to step in to help her since they were both capable of getting her down. But I had this sudden urge to feel her.

Together, we guided her down, the moment outwardly innocent. But the instant my hand brushed the curve of her hip, something dark and indulgent unfurled in my chest.

She turned her head slightly, eyes finding mine, and the look she gave me wasn't surprised. Like she had been expecting me to be there.

"Are they down?" she asked. Her voice was heavy with need.

"They are," I replied, my voice dropping without effort.

My fingers lingered, tracing a featherlight path along her bare arm. Deliberate. Unrushed. Her breath hitched, just enough to tell me she felt it too.

"We still have a few places left to—"

Her words died as I traced her bottom lip with my thumb. Somewhere between the twins' room and this spot, restraint had slipped its leash. I didn't give a damn about decorations anymore. The only thing I wanted to finish was her.

I didn't have to look at G. I felt him move.

He stepped in behind her, close enough that her back brushed his chest, caging her between us. We had always been like this, tuned to the same frequency, especially when it came to her. Tonight was no different.

"Carter..." she breathed, the sound soft and wrecked as my thumb slid to her neck.

"Yes, *Yume*?" I asked, already knowing why she'd said my name.

G fisted a handful of her locs and tipped her head back, sharp enough to make her pulse jump, gentle enough to remind her she was safe. That whatever we did next would be exactly what she wanted.

"Ah—" she gasped, cutting herself off. "No... we only have—"

We didn't let her finish.

Whatever she was about to say didn't matter unless it came out as a plea. I took her lips with mine while G licked and sucked on that beating pulse on her neck.

I marveled in the uncontrollable shutter of her body. Since reconnecting, we had come close many times to having her in the only way that could quench this insatiable hunger that I was somehow able to bury since the last time we had her.

I deepened our kiss, taking what I needed from her while simultaneously giving her everything I had. The kiss seemed to last forever, but it was only for a moment.

Like a well rehearsed dance, together, G and I turned her. She now faced him with her back to me. Pulling her to him, G took *Yume*'s lips with his hungrily. Almost like he was consuming her.

Somehow, we made it to the couch where we continued to devour her in various ways, still dressed, that had her panting and begging for us to take it further. That was how we wanted her.

Needy.

Wonton.

Dripping.

"Oh my, *Lykáki*, you're shaking," G taunted her as he ran his hand up and down her legging-covered legs.

"Gerasi—" she panted, but G cut her off.

"Shhh..." He hushed her. "Let us take care of you, baby."

A low whimper escaped her lips as he eased her pants down her thighs, and I began pulling her sports bra above her head. Her braless breasts fell heavy one by one, inviting me to take each into my mouth.

"Mmmm..." she moaned. "Carter."

I loved the sound of my name leaving her mouth. While giving her nipple the tongue lashing that was sure to have her peaking, I watched as the tip of her tongue ran across the top of her bottom lip, before pulling it between her teeth.

My dick swelled against the zipper of my slacks, begging me to free it. My mind went into that dark and heady place that yearned to feel her. To sink so deep into her that she was unsure where I started and she ended.

"You're so fucking wet, baby," G said in wonder.

There was no need for me to look for myself, I could smell how wet she was. I knew that she was more than wet; she was dripping.

Yume's hand drifted down her body, stopping just short of where she wanted us most, fingers curling like she was trying to decide whether to ask or take. Her breath was uneven now, eyes glassy, lips parted like she'd forgotten how to close them.

"Good girl." He praised her. "You know better than to touch yourself in our presence, *Lykáki*.

"Please," she begged, bucking her hips towards him.

I pulled away from her delectable nipples long enough to see G ghosting the outside of her lower lips, just barely slipping close enough to her inner folds.

Teasing.

Taunting.

"You want him to touch you, *Yume*?" I asked her, transfixed on the movement of G's finger, wanting desperately for it to be my tongue lapping at the honey that flowed from her.

"Tell us what you want," G followed. He allowed his finger to dip more into her wet falls, scooping up a puddle of her juices. "Gods, look at that."

As if he was talking to me, my eyes followed his hand. My mouth salivated seeing her essence drip down his fingers. Before it could be wasted, I caught a drop on my finger then lapped it up like it was communion.

The moment her taste touched my tastebuds, the small thread of sanity I had snapped. I pulled her up enough so that I could get underneath her.

"Ride my face," I demanded, turning her around so she straddled my lap.

I tapped her on the thighs to give her encouragement. She looked down from where she sat skeptically.

"I'm too—" she yelped when G slapped her ass hard enough to echo throughout the house.

"Did we ask if you were too fucking heavy, or did he tell you to get your sexy ass up there and ride his face?" G's command caused her to hurriedly straddle my face.

She had the perfect position. Her knees on both sides of my head, giving me a perfect view of the greatest gift created. Her pussy was indeed dripping, and the smell? *Kuso*, the smell was far better this close than when I caught a whiff.

Using two fingers, I parted her fat lower lips exposing her swollen bud that was jumping with need. With one fluid lick, I indulged in her taste, and if I thought that drop I took did me in, nothing compared to coating my tongue in her nectar.

"Fuckkk..." she gasped.

Normally, I would play with her. Bring her to the brink of ecstasy before backing off and having her writhing. But fuck the games.

I felt G settle behind *Yume*. He gripped her hips, careful not to break my connection to her. I was unable to see what he was doing exactly, but I had an idea.

Unbiddenly, we worked to feast on every part of her. I sucked her clit and lapped at the juices pouring from her while G moved from her pussy to her ass, working her until she was about to explode.

Yume bucked her hips wildly, and we kept up the pace effortlessly. She gripped a handful of my curls, using them as an anchor while she rode.

"Oh...my...g—" *Yume*'s screams were halted by the sound of the doorbell ringing.

We all paused and decided to ignore it. Whoever it was could either come back or leave.

Gripping her neck, I brought *Yume* back to the moment.

The bell rang again. Her head spun towards the foyer. G growled and stood from his spot on the floor, stomping for the door.

With a speed only a mother could possess, *Yume* was dressed back in her sports bra and reaching for the cardigan she left on the back of a chair. Unfortunately, that meant the mood was broken, yet again.

"I know, baby," she cooed, standing on her tiptoes, placing a kiss to my lips. "When whoever that is leaves, we can come back to this."

I huffed, rubbing my lips together. Her leftover essence on my lips flooded my tastebuds, pissing me off more than I already was. Whoever was at that door clearly had a death wish.

"I don't give a fuck who you are. Get the fuck off my property so I can go back to fucking my woman!" G roared.

We couldn't hear the person's response, but I knew if I didn't get to the door and do my job as the more reasonable of us two, we would cause our children more damage.

The sound of G's gun cocking sped up my movements. We were steps away when the person on the porch spoke, causing me to stop mid-step. *Yume* was walking right behind me, and my abrupt stop had her clashing into my back.

"Carter, are you okay?" she asked, placing a delicate hand on my shoulder.

"I'm not gonna repeat myself," G growled.

"Listen." Her thick accent flowed through the door, hitting me in my chest. "I do not give a damn who you are, *gigante*. I won't waste time repeating myself. Just know before you could even flex your finger, you'll be dead on this porch."

Yume ran the rest of the way to the door, jumping in front of G, between him and our uninvited visitor.

"Woahh, woahh! Let's all calm down," Yume said calmly. "My apologies about him. Is there something I can help you with, ma'am? Do you have car trouble?"

Yume asked her because the house G and I found for us was set back on more than ten acres of land and nothing but wooded area around it. Someone coming to our doorstep would mean either they meant to come here or that they needed help.

"Trouble? Ay, trouble is always at my heels." She laughed her answer to *Yume*. "*Pero* no, I am not currently here because of trouble. I am here because my son refuses to answer my calls or respond to my texts. So, here I am."

Claro removed the sunglasses. Her golden hazel eyes were a mirror to mine and our son caused *Yume* to gasp.

Dragging a hand down my face, I ground my back molars.

"Holy shit!" *Yume* shouted. "Carter, is this your mom?"

Loralei

I'd stared in the eyes of my son every day since the moment my birth doula placed him in my arms. It shocked me how identical they were to his father's. How much he shared many of his features. When I looked at her face, at her eyes, it was like looking at a female version of my son.

"Holy shit! Carter, is this your mom?" I was shocked.

Granted, I truly still knew little to nothing about these men. Majority was all learned in the last two weeks. I knew his mother was Latina, but I had no clue what she looked like. I just gathered they didn't have the best of relationships.

"*Sí*, I am, you are?" The question wasn't rude, just curious.

"Oh, my apologies." I held my hand out. "I'm Lor—"

"Why are you here, Claro?" Carter cut me off with a growl, pushing me behind him.

Gerasimou caught me as I lost my footing from the sudden move. "Carter, what the fuck?!"

He didn't answer me or look my way. His gaze was laser focused on the beautiful woman who didn't look old enough to have a son Carter's age.

"*Contéstame*," he demanded.

The sound caused me to jump, but his mom didn't even flinch. In fact, she looked uninterested by his outbursts.

"If I may come in, we can talk, *hijo*," she said softly.

"No."

"Hell no," Carter and Gerasimous said at the same time.

"Yes, you may." I moved around Carter then turned to look at them like they had lost their mind. It was a damn winter blizzard happening outside, and they had this woman standing on the porch refusing her.

"*Yume...*"

"*Lykáki...*"

They both growled. But I ignored them.

Walking around them both, I went right up to Claro and took her hand in mine. "Come in out the cold."

Together, we walked into the house, and I shot the men a dark look, and they met me with an even darker one. I knew there was more to the story of why Carter was so hostile with his mother and why she showed up unannounced. Like her son, I knew nothing about her other than her son, Javier, took my children after pretending to be someone else to me for months. And when I first found out I thought she had something to do with it, but call me crazy. Her aura told me she was a good woman. I also gathered she made some mistakes in her life, and the look in her eyes let me know she wanted to atone for them.

"Would you like something to drink? Water? Tea? I have coffee as well." I asked her.

"She doesn't need anything, she isn't staying long," G barked.

Ignoring him, I smiled at Claro waiting for her answer.

"*Gracias, querida*. If you do not mind, I will take a *Cafecito*, if that isn't too much."

"No, not at all. Is there a specific way you would like it?"

She scrunched her small nose and pursed her lips in thought. "Do you know what a *tino* is?"

I laughed. "I do. It's actually how Carter likes his coffee."

Surprise covered her face, but she masked it quickly. "Oh," she attempted to sound unaffected. "It is a very popular *café* in Colombia."

I gave her another smile squeezing her hand reassuringly. There was something about her that made my heart squeeze. I didn't know why Carter and his mother didn't have a relationship or why he held so much animosity in his heart towards her.

Honestly, it wasn't my business, but if we were going to do this with each other, all three of us giving this thing a go, then they were going to have to trust me and allow me to step in and be there for them.

Busying myself with making Claro her coffee, I didn't hear when one of them walked into the kitchen.

The house that they rented for us was an old farmhouse. I could tell the owners had done a lot of work on it but kept a lot of the older charm. Like having separate rooms in the house. The kitchen had a large arched doorway from the living room, giving it the open feel but still also giving it a separated one.

"Are you going to just stand there glaring at me?" I tossed over my shoulder but didn't turn around.

"What the hell are you doing, *Yume*?" Carter gritted.

"Nope."

"Nope? What do you mean nope?" his voice darkened.

"As in no. As in, you have me completely fucked up coming in here pointing any animosity towards me. As in, you better take that bass out of your voice. As in, you better go take a fucking walk before I walk my foot up your ass. That is the nope I mean," I told him calmly while continuing my task of making his mother's coffee.

The kitchen fell silent. They had heard me snap before but never in this manner. However, I was not now, nor would I ever, accept disrespect.

Carter took an audible breath before coming up behind me, slid my cardigan to the side and kissed my exposed shoulder. Even though he had irritated me, I shuddered involuntarily.

"*Los siento, Yume-chan.*" Carter spoke softly near the shell of my ear. "It was dishonorable of me to speak to you the way I had."

Turning to him, I gave him my attention. The instant our eyes met, the annoyance I felt towards him melted. Not because I condoned it but because I saw in his eye what he was attempting to hide behind the anger.

"Javone," I said again, quieter this time, my thumb brushing just beneath his eye. The word wasn't comfort so much as recognition. An acknowledgment of something old and tender I was only beginning to understand.

His jaw tightened under my hand. He didn't pull away. He didn't lean in either. He just stayed still, like he was deciding what to do with the moment.

Like he didn't want to even allow just how much his mom being here opened wounds he didn't want to explore.

"Not now, Loralei." He peered into my eyes. "I just need to see what she wants and get her to leave. I'm sorry about my actions to you and the animosity I brought into our home."

When he said *our home*, it did something to me. Even though we got here in an untraditional way and experienced something that could have turned out far worse, I was basically floating on a cloud.

It had only been two weeks since we came home from Berlin, and it felt like we hadn't slowed down once. On the flight back, I'd stressed myself out trying to figure out where the twins and I would live now that we no longer had a home, but Gerasimou and Carter shut that down, quickly letting me know that when it came to us, they had it handled.

We were moved into this beautiful house that same day. And now, waking up here every morning, living this life, felt like something I never would've allowed myself to imagine four years ago.

They had been making up for the hurt they caused me then, and I had been doing my damnedest to not allow their past transgression to dictate whatever we were trying to grow.

"How about this," I said evenly. "We bring her the coffee and give her a chance to speak. Then if we don't like what she has to say, I'll shoot her."

That garnered a small chuckle from him. Satisfied, I turned back to my task of making his mother's coffee. He might not see it now, but he needed to have that conversation with her, just as much as she needed to have it with him.

If he wanted to show up as the father I knew he could be, he needed to face the things that would hold him back. Because even though I could feel myself falling for these men–hell, I might have already been there–I would always choose my children's mental and physical health first. I would remove them from anything that didn't serve them. No exceptions.

After setting Claro's coffee on a tray with a few *pan de yucas* that Carter made with Dream the other day, I left him in the kitchen with his thoughts hoping that he would open himself up to the possibilities of reconciliation with his mom.

Plus, the sooner we figured out what she came here to say, the sooner we could get back to them blowing my back out.

G

Growing up, I never had a family. The streets of Greece raised me while the woman who spat me out, did whatever the fuck she wanted. One day I was approached by this couple who were dressed in the finest clothing I had ever seen. They offered to take me home to feed me since they had found me digging in the garbage outside a restaurant. If I had people who gave a shit about me, they would have taught me that going with strangers was wrong.

However, my mother wasn't the role model type, and with her track record, the identity of my father would forever be unknown. So, I went with them thinking I finally lucked up.

I was only seven at the time. Nothing but skin and bones, dirty, starving. These people were like the gods themselves took pity on me and sent them to me. For the first few years, everything was better than I could have wished for. They treated me like a long-lost child, giving me everything I could ever want. They enrolled me in school, showered me with love, even gave me their last name.

Unfortunately, they also taught me the hard truth that nothing in this life was done for free. When they found me, I was already tall for my age, just horrifically skinny. But as the years went on living with them, I began to eat better and got into doing sports, which made my lanky frame start to fill out, and I started to look older than my age.

The night of my thirteenth birthday was the night that lesson was taught. My adoptive mother had come into my room, which didn't alarm me since it wasn't anything out of the ordinary, she had done so since they took me in. Reading me stories, helping me bathe, and giving me a massage to help me sleep.

That night was the first time she offered a massage in a while though, and I was happy because the nightmares of my childhood had been plaguing me. However, that massage was loaded, and before I knew it, my body reacted to her touches. She told me that it was normal for young boys to react to a beautiful woman like I had.

She explained how she knew from the moment she saw me on the street I would grow into a handsome man. My reaction confused me because as far as I was concerned, she was my *mamá.*

That was the first night of many, and until Carter saved me, there were others, and I was trained to find children my age or younger for their sick games. The entire thing put my distrust in people, especially anyone who thought of themselves as parents.

It was the very reason I stood watching this *kariόla* as Loralei and Carter went into the kitchen. I didn't trust her or her intentions. Not with my kids in the house.

She had one time to make a move, and I would end her before she could smell the coffee.

"You stare at me as if I've wronged you, Dimitri." Her knowing my first name should have surprised me, but I'd learned to expect the most from anyone.

"Why are you here?" I asked her with no attempt to mask my disdain.

She chuckled like I told a joke. "I like you, Dimitri."

"Lady, I don't give a fuck if you like me. The feeling isn't mutual," I growled.

She raised a brow to my declaration. It wasn't a surprised look, more like she was curious by my animosity. To be honest, I truly didn't give a shit how she felt. I wanted her gone.

"Again, and this is the last time I ask, why the *fuck* are you here?"

"And I already told you why. I wanted to speak to my son."

I chortled at her lame attempt to call Carter her anything. This woman hadn't been in his life most likely since she pushed him out her decrepit pussy. The audacity of motherfuckers thinking they could just pop up after being a ghost and call someone their son.

"Bi—"

"Alrighty, here is your coffee, and I also brought you some of the *pan de yucas.*" *Lykáki* interrupted me about to tell this bitch where the fuck she could go with that *my son* shit.

"Oh, *querida.*" She smiled brightly at her, and one would think she was being genuine. "How did you know *pan de yuca* was my favorite?"

"Really..." *Lykáki* dragged, looking over her shoulder at Carter.

Carter's face was blank, but I knew his nonchalant ass well enough to know he was fuming.

"Claro." He called her name, cold and indifferently.

Claro didn't respond to him. Taking her time, she lifted her cup leisurely and sipped whatever it was *Lykáki* brought her.

"*Querida*, this is so good! Did my son teach you to make this?" she asked.

"Yes, he—" *Lykáki* started but was cut off by Carter.

"Cut the small talk, Claro, why the fuck are you here?" Carter barked.

The ladies both ignored him continuing with their conversation. "Well, I can tell you're a brilliant woman with how well you learned to make it. I feel like I am back home at my favorite café. And this *pan*, *deliciosa*!"

"*Gracias*, Claro." *Lykáki* blushed.

They continued to talk like they were old friends. I looked over to Carter, more annoyed he was allowing his bitch of a mother to sink her claws into our woman.

He looked at me with a dark look in his eyes that told me he was about to explode. To be honest, I enjoyed this side of my brother. He was always so well controlled the majority of the time and needed to relax.

When I heard laughing come from where they were, an involuntary growl escaped me.

"Gerasimou, are you okay?" *Lykáki* asked.

"I will be when she speaks her piece and leaves." I gritted.

"And as I told you, Dimitri..." She nodded towards Carter. "I came to speak with my son, and I will not leave until I do."

"Then speak!" Carter roared.

"I would prefer if we spoke alone."

Carter laughed darkly. "That isn't happening. Whatever you need to say, you can say it to us together, or not at all."

Claro and Carter held each other's stares for what felt like an eternity. The tension in the room thickened with so many unspoken words. As much as I felt whatever she needed to say was utter bullshit, it wasn't my call to make, and maybe this was a chapter Carter needed to close.

I wasn't a man who cared much about the past, but if I had the opportunity to tell my birth mother she was a waste of fucking air, I would jump on it. Fortunately for me, the gods shined on me at some point, and the bitch was dead. My only regret was that I wasn't the thing that killed her.

"*Listo.*" She conceded after realizing Carter wasn't backing down. "I wanted to tell you how sorry I am in person, Javone. I know it is wrong of me to ask for you to forgive me. *Pero,* before you make the decision to continue to hate me, at the very least, hear me out."

She paused waiting for Carter to reply. When she realized he had no intention of doing so, she continued.

"I met your father young. Sixteen, to be exact. I was at boarding school in Europe, and your father was there too. Meeting him felt like my black-and-white world suddenly went full color. We connected instantly."

She paused, taking a careful sip of coffee, eyes distant for a moment.

"Everything went well until my father found out. He came to the school demanding I end it. I was already promised to another man, eight years older. Our fathers expected me to marry him when I graduated. I told him I no longer would do it, that I'd fallen in love and planned to be with your father. I had never seen your *abuelo* so furious, and even angry... it was never aimed at me. He slapped me so hard I spat blood. I was terrified.

"He said I would obey. That if I saw your father again, we would die, and he would make me watch him kill my mother first before he killed me. At the time, I didn't know your father was destined to be the next *Kumichō*. When I told him, your father wanted to fight back, but I couldn't risk it. I cut all contact for a month. Then I found out I was pregnant with you. We kept you, and your father paid the school director to keep my pregnancy secret. I managed to hide it when my father visited. The only person I told was my mother who came for your birth.

"We lived in the dorms until I graduated. That summer, we went to stay with your father in Japan. You were just over one. When my father summoned me back, I wanted to take you, but I knew it would cost us both our lives. To protect you, I left you with your father, planning to return. But your abuelo had other plans.

"Jorge came into my room, one night. He claimed it was his right as my husband. I fought. I screamed. He beat me. I had no choice. The next morning, I learned I had been married since I was fifteen. I was furious, but I kept visiting you secretly. Your father even bought a hidden house in Colombia so I could see you safely.

"One time, your father had to leave for a few days. We did everything we could in that short time. If I had known it would be the last, I would have done more. When I returned, I walked into the living room covered in photos of us. My father made his presence known. He forbade me from seeing you. Every attempt ended with death lurking around us. Finally, when I saw a photo of Jorge talking to you at school, I realized I had no choice. I complied. Even then your nanny, my aunt, sent me letters and photos of you, so I remained present in your life, even from a distance."

Claro's words settled in the room like ash after a fire. No one spoke. We let the moment exist without trying to tame it.

I believed she was telling the truth. I also believed that nothing should ever stand in the way of being a mother.

I would burn the world to keep my children safe. I would end anyone who threatened them, blood or not. There were no excuses where they were concerned.

To me, that made her weak.

I looked at Carter. His face gave nothing away, as controlled and unreadable as ever–a skill he'd perfected long before this moment. Survival had taught him well.

Lykáki was the opposite. Her eyes were glassy, her fingers wrapped tight around Claro's hand like she was holding the woman upright through sheer will alone.

"I'm not telling you this because I expect it to absolve me of the hurt I caused you, *hijo*," Claro continued quietly, roughly brushing away her tears. "I only wanted you to know that I didn't leave because I didn't love you. Even when I wasn't there, I never stopped being your mother. I stayed away because without a plan, there was no safe way to keep you near me. I couldn't risk it."

Silence settled over the room again.

"I'm so sorry you had to endure that, Claro," *Lykáki* said at last, her voice gentle but steady. "To have your choices taken from you like that is horrific. I was unraveling during the week my children were taken. I can't imagine surviving years of it."

"Thank you for your kindness, querida," Claro replied. "But it isn't necessary."

"You made choices," I stated flatly. "Some of them were forced. Some of them weren't. We understand your circumstances. But understanding isn't the same as excusing it. And let's not forget it was your son, Javier, who took our children. How is it we can even trust the bullshit you're saying right now?"

"You are right, and you can't, Dimitri. *Pero,* not because I had anything to do with his decisions but because in the life we all live, trust isn't something we should do lightly. I have to earn that trust. Furthermore, while Javier is my son, we do not have the best relationship. I've come to terms with the outcome of Javier's life."

I grunted, and Carter still hadn't moved. His face continued to be locked down so tightly it might as well have been carved from stone.

I nodded my head towards him. "I don't speak for him," I said, my voice lower now. "And I won't take this moment from him. But don't mistake his silence for forgiveness. If it was left up to me, your ass wouldn't even be in here."

Claro held my gaze, something unreadable flickering behind her eyes. Pain, maybe. Or resignation.

Before she could respond, the front door opened.

The sound cut clean through the room. Carter and I moved on instinct, guns drawn and aimed at the entryway.

No one spoke. We waited.

Carter's father stepped inside like he belonged there, wool coat dusted with fresh snow, boots tracking cold into the house. He didn't look surprised to see Claro. If anything, it felt expected.

For reasons I couldn't explain, his presence didn't shock me either.

Carter and I lowered our weapons. I wasn't afraid of him, but I understood power when I saw it. If Tahashi was here, he wouldn't have come alone.

"*Oyabun*," Carter said, bowing deeply.

"Takahashi," his father returned, just as measured.

"What brings you here, Father?" Carter asked, voicing what all of us already knew.

"He came with me," Claro said, rising as Tahashi moved toward her. "I asked you to wait in the car. I wanted to speak with him alone."

Carter

"And I told you, *Taiyo-chan*, I would give you no more than thirty minutes. I gave you thirty-three." I blinked rapidly at my father's softness.

In my entire life I had never seen this man be soft. Never seen him look at Claro the way he was. Not like she was the entire energy keeping his world alive.

The same way G and I looked at *Yume.*

"Are you alright?" he asked her, his leather-gloved hand brushing her cheek.

"I am," she said. The answer was steady, but the hurt threaded through it anyway.

My father turned toward me. Whatever softness he'd offered her disappeared, replaced by the cool, distant authority I knew too well.

"Did she tell you?" he asked.

"Hai." I nodded once.

"Then we move forward," he said, as if that settled everything. "We will be a family."

The words landed wrong. Too clean. Too easy.

"Where are my *magotachis*?"

The room went still.

Yume's expression shifted–not in confusion or fear. In offense. Her spine straightened, her grip tightening around the arm of the couch like she'd just been slapped with the audacity of him.

"Moving on as a family?" she repeated, quiet but sharp. "I'm sorry I don't mean any disrespect, but you don't get to decide that."

My father's gaze slid to her for the first time, like he just noticed she was here. *Yume* was now standing from where she sat on the couch

"You speak as if this concerns you."

"It does in fact concern me since you're standing in our house," she said, rising to her feet, voice calm but lethal. "And because you don't get to walk in here, erase decades of damage with a sentence, like you didn't have a hand in the trauma."

G shifted beside me. I felt it, the tension. The instinct to protect her if my father decided to react to her words.

"Your emotions change nothing,"' he stated calmly. "Takahashi needed to hear the truth of the event, so he may move past this nonsense. *Taiyo-chan* has provided him with it, so he should now let it go."

Yume scoffed. "Let it go?" She looked to me. "Do you want to let it go, Carter?"

Everyone turned to me. Before I could answer, my father spoke. "He will let it go. And you will shut your mouth and learn your place if you are to stand by my son's side."

"Shut my mouth?" Yume echoed, disbelief sharpening every syllable. "Motherfucker, do I look like someone who exists to be quiet for men who confuse authority with entitlement?"

The air went electric.

My father's jaw tightened. He wasn't used to resistance, not from women and certainly not when I was present. However, I had no intention of stopping *Yume*.

"I will forgive you for speaking out of turn," he said coolly. "It seems you have not been taught that a woman of your stature should be seen and not heard."

Yume let out a short, humorless laugh. "I don't know what in *The Handmaid's Tale* you think this is, but you can take that mindset and walk back out the door you came through if you're going to speak to me like that."

My father let out a laugh of his own. "Is this how you've trained your woman to speak? Either of you?"

"You know what, I've had enough of you talking to me like I am insignificant." *Yume* walked to stand between G and I. Together, the three of us stood a united front.

"*Aguanta*!" Claro stepped forward, planting herself firmly in the center of the living room. "We did not come here to disrespect Loralei. You have been nothing but kind to me since I arrived, and I apologize on our behalf for implying otherwise."

"Do not speak for me, *Taiyo-chan*," my father said flatly. "If this girl—"

"You have one more time to disrespect her, and I will forget you are my *Oyabun*." The faint click of G's Beretta punctuated the threat. I didn't want to go to war with my father, but behind Yume and her respect, I would crumble empires.

"You dare threaten me, Takahashi?" my father asked, head tilted, amusement in his voice.

"It wasn't a threat, motherfucker," G said evenly, his presence a wall of calm menace.

"Men!" Claro cut in again, voice sharp. "Listen, this has gone off course. Tahashi, enough. Out there, you are the feared leader of the Yakuza, *pero aquí*, among family, you are a father and a man with honor. So sit the hell down so we may speak to our son, Dimitri, and Loralei respectfully!"

Tahashi's eyes sharped on Claro, his posture rigid, but slowly, deliberately, he lowered himself on the couch. Claro didn't back down as she watched him lower into his seat. They shared a wordless conversation, and when she was satisfied, she turned back to us.

"*Los seinto* again, please accept my apology. I would like to please clear as much of the air. My..." She looked behind her to my father. "Our main goal this evening was to talk and to come to an understanding. We were not good parents to you, *hijo*. I know this. While we may have made decisions we thought best at the time, ultimately, it was at the cost of you. I can never change that nor will I try. I just want to have a chance."

I rolled her words in my mind. A part of me wanted to tell her and my father to leave my place of peace. To hold on to the hurt and anger I had become accustomed to. It was what built the man I was standing before them as.

On the other hand, I thought about what *Yume* said to me in the kitchen. Holding onto the anger did nothing for me, and even if unintentionally, it could be pushed to the twins. I couldn't call myself a man of honor who would do anything to protect his children if I wouldn't do the very thing that could make me not just better for them but for *Yume*.

I looked at her, and she gave me a small smile with a nod. I then looked to G, the one person who shared the pain of absentee parents, and while his body was on guard, I saw in his eyes the hurt that always lingered there. I saw it because it mirrored mine. How could I want for him to let go of his past and live but not do so myself?

Turning back to my parents, I met Claro's gaze. "Why now?" I asked.

She closed her eyes, took a shaky breath, and opened them slowly, the faintest tremor in her lips betraying the calm she tried to project. "Because I owed it to you. Because for years I let my father dictate my life, and in doing so, you almost lost your children. The guilt I carried... it ate at me every day, Javone. I've spent my life building an empire, surviving threats from my father and Jorge, and if I had trusted your father to not just protect me, but to help me finally do what was right, we wouldn't be here. I was terrified of rejection, of retaliation—but more than anything, you deserved the truth. All of it."

On her last sentence, she stepped closer, reaching her small hand to my face.

Until Yume, I had never known softness like this. I thought I'd pull away, but instead, I found myself leaning into her touch. Her palm was warm, delicate, insistent in a way that felt like it had been missing from my life. Every nerve in me recognized it, and something inside me that I thought long dead stirred awake.

"I love you, hijo, and I am sorry I failed you as a mother. I can only pray that you not only forgive me but allow me a place in your life."

I didn't answer. I just stared, and for the first time, let the anger I carried loosen, even if just a fraction. Her eyes held nothing but truth and regret, and somehow that made it enough.

"Great!" My father's voice cut through, clapping his hands. The spell of the moment shattered instantly, but even as he did, the heat of her touch lingered.

"I am happy that we could work through this," *Yume* beamed. Like just minutes ago she wasn't ready to go toe for toe with my father. "I was about to make dinner. The twins will be up soon, and I would love for you to meet them."

Claro and my father shared a look. I couldn't read it, but I felt there was more they needed to say.

"We would love to, *pero,* would you be able to accommodate for two additional settings?" Claro asked.

Yume looked to me uncomfortably before looking back to Claro. "Um, yes. I was going to make soup and arepas."

"Who are the other two guests?" G asked.

I hadn't said anything because I wasn't sure I wanted to know the answer.

"We didn't want to really spring it on you and hoped that we could ease it in..." Claro rushed to explain.

"Spring... what?" I asked, trying to reign in my annoyance at yet another secret.

"Your sisters," my father said. "Julieta and Jessenia. They have been waiting in the car."

I blinked rapidly at my father's revelations. *I have sisters.*

Loralei

Christmas Day

"Wolfie, please get your hands away from that table!" I scolded my son for what felt like the millionth time.

He and his sister had been running through the house like tiny hurricanes, fingers grabbing at anything within reach. I'd already warned his greedy little behind more times than I could count to leave the food table alone, but today, he was committed to exercising his right to selective hearing.

"Wolfe."

Gerasimous's voice boomed through the room.

That did the trick. My boy straightened instantly, hand freezing mid-reach as he slowly turned toward his dad. His shoulders squared like he'd just been called into a meeting he definitely wasn't prepared for.

"Otay, Dada," he mumbled, dropping his hand and his head.

My heart ached seeing my baby so dejected. He was only being a three-year-old, and while he needed to leave the food alone, it still tugged at me. I'd already had to replace three of the appetizers I set out, and it wasn't even noon yet.

"No yell at Woflie, Dada!" Dream came barreling into the dining room like a tiny wrecking ball.

She went straight to her brother, planting herself in front of him with a deep scowl. "You 'tay, Wolfie?" she asked, rubbing his back like she was the older sibling instead of his twin.

Wolfe nodded once, still sulking.

I saw the exact moment her little protection act got to G. His shoulders dropped just a fraction, his jaw relaxed, and he sighed heavily.

I was no stranger to them pulling this card, so I turned and went back into the kitchen, leaving him to deal with the fallout.

It was Christmas Day, and we were expecting a house full of guests. My first time hosting anything like this, and I was already overwhelmed. There was food to finish, timing to keep, and about a thousand ways this could go wrong if I let myself spiral.

Having the twins hopped up on sugar from the candy in their stockings wasn't helpful in the least. The ding of the oven timer went off, and I excitedly opened it to check the prime rib.

As soon as it opened, the delicious smell hit me, making my stomach growl. Stupidly, I hadn't eaten yet today. The twins had us up before the sun screaming about Santa leaving them 'pwesents'. Since then, it'd been nonstop going.

Carter and Gerasimou bought the twins so much stuff I genuinely wondered if any online store had inventory left afterward. Wolfe's favorite gift was the massive collection of monster trucks, especially the one big enough for him to ride in. He'd been circling it all morning like it might disappear if he blinked too long.

Dream, on the other hand, had been in absolute doll-baby heaven from the moment she ripped open her first box. The squeal that tore out of her was sharp, joyful, and so full, it lodged itself straight into my chest. That sound alone made every ounce of stress worth it.

It wasn't that I couldn't afford to give them nice things. I could. I had more money than I honestly knew what to do with. My babies had never wanted for anything. But this… this was different. The scale of it. The intention behind it. And now that they were older, now that they understood Christmas, it hit harder.

Their joy was visible.

"It smells good in here, biiitch!"

I whipped around, letting out a squeal of my own at the sound of my best friend's voice.

"Cheeellllee!"

I took off toward her like a woman possessed. We collided in a hug that damn near knocked us both off balance, like we hadn't seen each other in years when it'd only been a month.

"Best friennnd!" she yelled, squeezing me tight.

I pulled back just enough to look at her. "I am so happy you're here."

She blinked at me like I'd lost my mind. "It's Christmas. Where else would I be?"

Before I could respond, she leaned past me, eyes going wide as she took in all the twins' gifts as they played with her youngest daughter two years older than them. The wrapping paper carnage. The toys. The ride-on truck Wolfe was currently riding throughout the open space. Carter had moved the large sofa in the family room to give them full use of the large space.

"Oh, hell no," she breathed. "Did y'all rob Santa?"

I laughed. "Feels like it."

Her gaze softened as Dream toddled past us clutching a doll almost as big as her torso. "Look at them," Chelle mused. "They look happy."

"They are," I said quietly.

She looked back at me then, really looked. "And so do you."

I didn't answer right away. Just smiled. "I am."

"So, these are the infamous men that knocked my bestie up with a phenomenon, huh?" she questioned, bumping me with her shoulder. "I bet that's why you in here glowing... they must be knocking them cobwebs out ya—"

"Chelle!" I cut her off.

"What?" She had the nerve to act shocked.

I was about to tell her how nasty her ass was, but the doorbell saved us both. The guys were busy playing with the kids, so I answered it.

The moment I opened the door, Jessenia practically yelled, "Merry Christmas!" while Julieta stood behind her grinning like she'd been waiting all day.

"Merry Christmas," I replied, giving her a hug.

They were the only ones at the door. "Where is everyone else?" I asked.

They both looked behind them to the black SUV that stuck out in the heavy snowfall.

"On business calls as always," Jessenia answered, rolling her eyes.

"Don't start, Jessie," her sister chastised.

I smiled as they started to bicker before I guided them into the house.

"Tee Yessiee!"

"Tee Ulieee!"

Dream and Wolfe squealed and launched themselves across the room like tiny missiles the second they spotted their aunts. Wrapping paper crunched under their feet as they barreled forward, arms outstretched.

"Oh my God." Julieta laughed, crouching down just in time to catch Dream. "I missed you, *mi corazón*."

Wolfe skidded to a stop in front of Jessenia, arms wide. "Up!"

Jessenia scooped him up with ease, pressing noisy kisses into his cheeks until he squealed. "How are you heavier already, *gordito*?" she teased, tickling him until he kicked his feet. "What are they feeding you over here?"

Carter stood a few feet away, arms crossed, trying not to stare while absolutely staring. Gerasimou was beside him, solid and quiet, like he always was. They'd both been there when Carter met his sisters for the first time days ago. Both of them standing in the doorway while his whole world shifted.

Finding out he had sisters had been a shock on its own. Finding out they were fifteen, sharp-mouthed, opinionated, and completely uninterested in tiptoeing around his feelings had been something else entirely.

They hadn't treated him like a stranger or a secret.

They treated him like a brother.

No hesitation. No awkward distance. Just immediate familiarity, teasing him, questioning him, claiming him like he'd always been theirs. Whatever confusion Carter had been holding onto, they burned right through it.

And they'd taken to Gerasimou just as easily. He came to the foyer pulling their attention from the twins who were animatedly telling them about every toy they received.

"Dimitri!" Julieta said, already moving.

Before he could brace himself, both of them wrapped their arms around him, hugging him tight like they'd been doing it their whole lives. Gerasimou froze for half a second, still not used to so much unburdened affection, then exhaled and hugged them back, one hand resting carefully on each of their shoulders.

Jessenia pulled back just enough to grin up at him. "Merry Christmas, Dimitri."

Gerasimou stepped back making room for their brother, who they wasted no time colliding into him with hugs.

"Merry Christmas, *oniichan*!" they said in chorus.

"Merry Christmas, Jessi-chan." He kissed the top of Jessenia's head then turned to Julieta. "Merry Christmas, Juli-chan."

The girls beamed under their brother's affection. The same way the twins bombarded them when they came in, the girls did the same with a rapid fire of their last few days to not only Carter but also to Gerasimou.

While they were talking, the door opened to Claro and Tahashi coming in looking like a regal boss couple. Claro immediately hugged me, telling me how beautiful I looked. Tahashi gave me a small smile before following Claro to where Carter and Gerasimou were speaking to their daughters. I was about to close the door but was stopped by a man's shoe.

"Excuse me," I snapped, instantly going on alert.

The man didn't say anything but also didn't make his way into the house.

"Oh, *quierda*, he is with us. They are bringing in the gifts," Claro informed me.

Nodding, I stepped out the way and watched as three men came in carrying what felt like endless boxes and bags. Claro directed them to the living room where the twins had run off to with Chelle's two kids.

"Alela! Alelo!" the twins screeched for the millionth time today.

It was wild how quickly the twins latched onto them and vice versa. If you weren't in this world, you would not have guessed that Tahashi was the fearsome leader of the Yakuza or that Claro was the *Jefa* of a dangerous cartel.

They got right down on the floor with the kids playing. Claro crawled around along Wolfe, with her silk double pleated pants sweeping the floor without a care in the world. And Tahashi was laid out on the floor pretending to be a patient as Dream and Lila, Chelle's daughter, performed a surgery on him.

The doorbell rang again.

Then again.

At some point, within a short time, the house was full. When we first moved in here, I was concerned with how much space there was, but truly if this was what holidays were going to be like, then I hoped our forever home would be this big.

Once the last of our guests—Finlay and Banks—showed up, I called everyone to the dinner table. The kids, including Jessenia and Julieta, since the twins begged them, had their own table in the breakfast nook. Gerasimou set it up, plates and all, like a tiny adults' replica. The adults settled around the ridiculously long table that fit all fifteen of us comfortably.

We ate together, talking over each other, laughing at dumb jokes, passing dishes back and forth. The smell of the food, the warmth of the house, the noise of little feet running through the kitchen, everything felt... normal. So damn normal, I had to remind myself to breathe. I hated to sound like a broken record, but for years, I truly I never thought I'd see this happen.

Carter was quieter than usual, but I could see it in the way he glanced at the twins, who were holding court with their aunts. Every time Wolfe laughed at something Julieta said, or Dream leaned into Jessenia, Carter would smile, just a little. It was subtle, but I saw it.

Gerasimou was at my side, watching the room. He gave me a look every now and then, feeding me something off his plate, talking with Riker and bickering with Smalls.

Claro and Tahashi were talking with my parents who sat across from them, like old friends. While my sister continued to try and act like Banks wasn't her man. Chelle and James were talking with Finlay, Kilter, and Peace.

Shortly after dinner, the adults began drifting toward the extra bedrooms upstairs I had made for them. The farmhouse was warm and full, the faint smell of roasted vegetables still lingering, and I was wiped out. It was a good night but still a lot.

I caught Wolfie rubbing his tired eyes. Chelle had long taken her kids up to bed, and it was that time for mine as well.

"Okay, my babies, it's time for bed," I announced, starting to stand u p.

Julieta beat me to it, scooping up a yawning Dream. "We can put them to bed," she offered.

"Are you sure?" Carter asked.

"Putting these little storm cells to bed can be a task," Gerasimou added.

"We're sure." Jessenia smiled, picking up Wolfie. "Come on, *chiquitines*, let's get you to bed."

"No bed!" Wolfe started to protest, wiggling in her arms.

"If you let us get you to bed, you can sleep with me and 'Ulie," Jessenia bribed him. That was all my boy needed to sharpen right up.

The girls set the twins down, and they ran to us with quick hugs and kisses before allowing their aunts to carry them up to their bedroom.

The last to go were our parents. My mom and dad came over to me pulling me from the couch into a hug, tightly.

"This may not be how we would have picked love for you," my mom whispered in my ear, "but I watch them with you, I know you're in great hands."

She squeezed my arm gently and moved to give my dad a chance. "Lolo," he started. "Thank you for dinner. Get some sleep, baby girl.

We got the kiddos in the morning." He kissed my forehead before leaving out the back door with my mother.

Carter's mom pulled me into a hug next, and then surprisingly, so did his father. Since the day he busted his way into my house and was rude as hell, I wasn't expecting us to be on that level anytime soon. Not to mention he didn't seem like the affectionate type. And although it was awkward, I returned the hug.

"Thank you so much for tonight and allowing us to stay as well," he said.

"Yes, *quierda*," Claro added. "I enjoyed myself. Please rest in, tomorrow we will take care of the babies. Ooo... maybe I will cook you all breakfast."

I just smiled and nodded. I doubted the twins would let me sleep in but appreciated both theirs and my parents' offers.

"You ready for bed, baby?" Carter asked me.

I nodded, too tired to speak. Gerasimou noticed and picked me up over his shoulder. He rubbed my butt, giving it a gentle squeeze that did more waking me up than relaxing. When he kissed the exposed part of my thigh, I damn near melted into him.

Carter stepped to meet my face, landing a gentle kiss to my lips. "Shower, then bed, *Yume*," he scolded me . I wanted to protest, but truly, cuddling with my men sounded like everything.

Loralei

Something felt good.

Too damn good for a dream.

I was deep under, but something was pulling me out of it. My mind was foggy, like I was still tangled in the silk of a good dream, but my brain had started lighting flares, urging me to come back to the land of the living.

I didn't remember much, just bits and flashes.

A wild, beautiful Christmas.

The house filled with noise, heat, and family.

Love everywhere, even with so much still unresolved.

The twins running wild, toys scattered across the floor, giggles bouncing off the walls. It was chaotic. It was perfect.

The guys had carried me to bed. I'd wanted them to fuck me into the next dimension, but they were on a different mission. Shower. Rest. Recharge. Gerasimou ran a bath in the biggest damn tub I'd ever seen, bigger than the one we had at the Colorado cabin. Carter stripped me, and when the water was ready, he eased me down into it.

They took turns—one massaging, one pouring steaming water down my back. My skin sang for it. When it was Gerasimou's turn, his hands hit a spot in my shoulders that made me melt. I let out this breathless moan without even meaning to, and then... nothing.

I blacked out.

Wake up, Loralei!

My eyes shot open.

That big motherfucker put me to sleep. Again.

And here I was thinking we'd grown, learned something. Communicated. So, what the hell was the point of kidnapping me if we were just gonna repeat the same old shit?

Then I heard it. Slurping. Wet, messy, intentional.

My senses sharpened fast. I blinked a few times, confused—then froze.

Between my legs, waves of dark hair I knew better than my own reflection.

"Gerasimou..." I moaned, my back arching involuntarily.

He didn't answer. Instead, he slid his large hand up my belly and pressed me down like he knew I'd try to run. His other hand moved between my thighs, and two thick fingers pushed inside me like they belonged there.

"Fu—" I gasped. Just two, and I was already full.

"Gods. You. Taste. So. Good. Lykáki," he groaned against my pussy. Each word vibrated through me like a low growl.

If there was an award for best pussy eater, Gerasimou had that shit in the bag. No competition. The way he sucked and licked while fucking me with those thick fingers... it was deliberate. Focused. He knew exactly what would rip me apart and put me back together.

My walls started to clamp around him, pulsing tight every time he curved his fingers just right. My orgasm was right there. I could feel her coming up my spine, almost close enough to grab.

But just before I could tip over, he changed the rhythm. Inside me. On my clit. Everything shifted.

"Please... don't stop," I begged, voice thin, strung out.

He ignored me and kept moving slower, letting me build again before twisting away at the last second.

I started bucking, chasing the orgasm he kept snatching away. Reaching down, I attempted to grab at his head, trying to force him deeper into my honey pot, but my wrist was caught in something.

What the fuck?

Were my hands tied?

"G...Gera...fuck..." I tried to ask him, but he was eating me so good, I couldn't get a single coherent thought out.

He sucked me harder like he was trying to find the center of my tootsie pop, and I swear if he kept this up, he'd get a gusher instead.

His fingers curled again, deeper this time. My thighs trembled. My stomach caved.

The door opened on a quiet creek. I didn't have to look to know who it was. I felt the air in the room shift. It was one thing to have one of them in a confined space, but when they both were, it felt like they sucked all the air and every coherent thought from my mind.

Gerasimou didn't stop as Carter stood there in the doorframe watching as his head stayed deep between my legs, sucking and licking. He had removed his fingers, and my pussy clenched desperately in their absence.

I blinked through the tears pooling at the corners of my eyes.

Carter stepped inside without a word.

I tried to say something. I couldn't. My mouth opened, but no sound came out. My body was too close. Every nerve drawn to where Gerasimou was still working me open, deliberately, without pause.

Carter's eyes moved, following the drag of Gerasimou's tongue, the slow curl of his fingers as he gripped me by my hips, the tremble in my thighs. He didn't say a thing. Just watched it all.

He came to the side of the bed, stood there for a beat, then reached down, brushing his knuckles across my cheek.

I leaned into the touch without meaning to.

"Breathe," Carter said.

I tried... like really fucking tried, but it was like my body was incapable of inhaling.

"I...I.." I couldn't even speak.

Reaching down, Carter slowly trekked his way to my breast, giving it a rough squeeze. The pressure from it did more to me than it made sense.

Again, I arched, and this time no one pushed me down. "Uhh..." I moaned.

My chest rose and fell rapidly.

I couldn't breathe.

Chest fluttering, head swimming, nerves too loud, too much. My thighs shook. My arms were useless, bound above me, twitching with every flick of Carter's fingers on my nipples.

Gerasimou didn't stop, grip bruising my hips as his mouth worked me, and Carter's hand slid from my breast to my throat.

He didn't squeeze, not really, he only pressed enough to remind me I belonged to him.

My breath stopped completely.

My eyes flew to his. Wide. Wild. I was floating and pinned at the same time.

His thumb slid under my jaw.

"Breathe," he said again.

I couldn't. His hand was right there. But then... Gerasimou's mouth shifted. His tongue flattened, pressing hard against my clit, exactly where I needed it. His fingers returned, two of them pushing deep, curling just right, relentless. Like he'd found the blueprint of my body and decided to exploit every nerve.

My hips lifted before I could stop myself. Carter's hand held my throat, steadying me right on the edge, and something in me gave way in that exact moment. I pulled in a breath, shaky and sharp, like it was the first real one I'd taken in hours. My thighs clamped around Gerasimou's head, but he didn't budge, only groaning into me like he wanted to drown there.

Carter leaned in, his lips by my ear.

"Now."

That single word hit me harder than anything else.

My body shattered.

My orgasm tore through me so hard it knocked the air right back out. I cried out—raw, loud, helpless. My vision blurred. My fingers curled against the restraints, wrists aching, toes pointed, thighs trembling.

They held me through it.

Carter's hand drifted from my neck to my lower belly, pressing me back as Gerasimou licked me through the aftershocks. I didn't even know if I was shaking or crying or both.

I only knew I could finally fucking breathe.

G

There was nothing fucking sexier than watching Lykáki cum. Watching her lose control, break apart beneath us, unravel without shame. I could live off the sight of her like that. If the gods ever took it from me, I'd burn the fucking sky to get it back.

My dick throbbed behind my zipper, thick and aching, ready to slide into the only place that'd ever felt like home. Tight. Wet. Mine.

She was trembling on the bed, chest rising too fast, face flushed. My beard was dripping with her. She'd come so hard it left her whole body vibrating.

I was supposed to take my time.

We were going to tease her. Make it last. Stretch it out slowly and carefully because it had been so long since I'd felt her, felt this. Waiting those four years felt like fucking torture.

Having her like this tied up, with every distraction taken care of, I was done waiting.

I stood, unzipped, and let my dick fall free. I was so hard it hurt, leaking at the tip, my whole body tight with it.

Carter looked over at me. His hand stayed flat on her chest, grounding her. He didn't say anything. He didn't have to.

I climbed onto the bed, lined myself up, and dragged the head of my dick through the slick mess between her legs. She twitched under me, hips jerking, desperate for more.

I gripped her thigh, held her still.

"You want slow?" I asked, voice low.

She blinked up at me, lips trembling. "I want *you*."

That was all I needed to hear.

I pushed in deep, slow, only because her body was so tight it demanded it. Her heat wrapped around me instantly, gripping me like she didn't want to let go.

How was she so fucking tight after all this time? After birthing two kids?

My head dropped back. "Fuuuckkkk."

The thought of her—swollen, pregnant, full of me—hit my brain like a fucking freight train. I shoved deeper. Had to stop, hold still, or I was gonna cum too fucking fast.

She was gripping the ropes, her mouth open like she didn't even know how to close it.Her eyes fluttered, cheeks flushed, while I slid in all the way, stretching her open.

Then Carter moved.

His body shifted over hers, smooth as ever, and without a word, he tapped the head of his dick against her lips. Not rough. Just enough to claim her attention.

"Lick them," he said, calm like he was asking for tea.

And because she was a good fucking girl, she did. Her tongue slipped out, soft and wet, tracing over her plump lips and the tip of his dick like she was tasting something sacred. Her lips parted after, hungry and pretty.

Carter didn't make her wait. He pushed into her mouth with a steady roll of his hips. She opened wide, cheeks hollowing, suction tight like she was trying to pull the soul out of him.

Watching her like that, with his dick in her mouth and mine still buried inside her pussy, was enough to short-circuit every logical thought I had left.

Carter started to move, thrusting into her mouth like he was training her all over again.

I picked up the rhythm. When he slid in, I pulled out. When I pushed in, he drew back. We continued smoothly, alternating who did what.

Her body rocked between us, tied down, dripping, spit leaking from the corners of her mouth just like it was dripping out of her pussy.

We had her soaked at both ends.

I looked down at where we were combined. Her pussy was gripping me so tight, its creamy wetness coating me. Her clit was swollen, twitching like it was begging to be touched again.

I slapped it.

Once. Then again.

Her pussy juices coated my fingers, and like an addict, I hurriedly stuffed them into my mouth sucking them clean.

She jerked under me, choking around Carter's dick. Her throat flexed. She moaned, tried to keep sucking even while she writhed.

We picked up speed, still slow but a bit faster, and I tried to push so deep inside of her that she'd end up choking on both of us.

She was a fucking mess—tied up, mouth stretched wide around Carter's dick, her body limp and used and still so goddamn hungry. Her pussy gripped me like it didn't want to let go, clenching every time

I bottomed out. The wet sounds between us were obscene, echoing off the walls like music.

"Fuck, baby, you feel so fucking good," I groaned, losing myself.

Normally, I kept quiet during sex. Never felt the need to talk.

But with her, with *Lykáki,* I couldn't hold it in. I needed her to know what she did to me. How fucking addictive it was having her wrapped around my dick while I could still smell her on my face, her taste still thick on my tongue.

She moaned in response. Whether it was to what I said or the way Carter was gripping both sides of her head and using her throat like his personal fuck toy, I didn't know.

Didn't care.

Either way, we kept at it with a slow, perfect rhythm that made my spine tighten with every stroke.

The feeling was too fucking good. I shoved deeper before I even realized I was doing it and had to hold still just to keep from cumming like a fucking teenager.

"Shit—" I muttered, closing my eyes.

No longer able to hold back, I snatched out of her, I pulled out fast, grabbed my dick, and stroked once, twice, until I was spilling all over her. Thick, hot ropes of cum painted her pussy, her belly, her thighs. Then I rammed back into her to finish, hoping I'd get the chance to watch a baby grow in her this time.

She made a soft, strangled noise like feeling my cum on and in her wrecked her in the best way.

I stood there for a second, breathing hard, watching her tremble with Carter still deep in her throat.

She was messy and ruined and perfect.

Mine.

Ours.

And we weren't even done yet.

Carter

Sex with Yume was always... otherworldly. Since we came back from Berlin, we had made every attempt to reconnect like this, but something always pulled at our attention. Not danger, not chaos, just life.

Life filled now with our children, family, and no.

This time, we made sure nothing stood in our way.

The moment both sets of parents offered to wake up with the twins so she could sleep in, I knew exactly what I wanted. And when my sisters insisted the twins stay curled up with them for the night, it sealed it. The house was still, quiet in the way that only came when everyone else was watching out for what mattered most.

Watching her choke and gag on my member was a sight I'd waited too long to see again. No matter how far I pushed into her greedy mouth, she took it. Tears streaked down her face, spit shining on her lips, her throat working hard around me without hesitation.

When I finally came, it hit me harder than expected, deeper. Like something I'd been holding back for years finally let go. If I was honest, I hadn't felt release like that since the last time I was buried deep inside her.

I reached into my back pocket, took out the blade, and cut the ties from her wrists.

Her arms dropped immediately, body sank into the bed like gravity had finally claimed her. She didn't even try to move, just laid there spent.

I took that moment to really look at her.

Every naked inch of her.

My release at the corner of her lips. G's release coating her thighs and the soft curve of her belly. The subtle changes motherhood had etched into her body. Not flaws, but proof.

She didn't even seem to realize G had carried her from our room to here. She just let it happen, trusting us to handle the rest.

I sat back, hand resting on her stomach without thinking.

This body had carried our children, had stretched, endured, healed. And the thought hit me so sharply, it stole my breath.

I wanted her pregnant again.

Not someday. Not as an idea. Now.

The need settled low and heavy. Not frantic. Not wild. Certain.

I leaned back against the pillows and looked at her.

"Come here," I said quietly.

Her eyes opened, tired, soft, but hungry.

She didn't hesitate.

Even exhausted, she pushed herself up and crawled toward me. Her movements were slow, but eager. Purposeful. She climbed over my thighs, wrapped her hand around me, and lined herself up like she'd done it a thousand times before.

Then she sank down.

Slow. Deep.

Her breath caught. Mine did too.

"Carterrr…" she whispered, voice already wrecked, still sensitive from everything her last orgasm.

I gripped her hips and held her there, feeling her body settle around me. Feeling how warm she was. How tight. How ready.

"That's it," I murmured. "You're perfect like this."

She rolled her hips carefully at first, testing the stretch, her forehead dropping to my chest. I guided her, keeping the pace deep and steady.

"Yes, *Yume*," I said as I bit my bottom lip. "Ride me."

It was like she'd been waiting to hear it.

She moved with more confidence then, lifting and sinking, her body remembering exactly how to take me. Her breath broke every time she bottomed out, her walls fluttering around me like they were welcoming me back.

Behind her, the bed shifted.

G's hands came down on her hips, heavier than mine, spreading her open, anchoring her. She whimpered, the sound sliding straight through me.

"You look unfucking real like this," he murmured, voice rough with heat. "Watching you take him while I'm right here…your ass begging for me. Fuck. You want me in your ass, baby?"

She shuddered. The only answer he needed.

I kept my hands steady on her waist. "You're doing so good, baby."

G's fingers traced lower, slow, deliberate. She tensed around me. He lined himself up behind her and pushed in slowly, stretching her open inch by inch. She gasped, her whole body tightening as she adjusted to both of us.

"Relax, *Yume*," I coached her while spreading her ass cheeks open. "Let him in."

She nodded, breath shaking.

"Fuck," he breathed. "You feel incredible."

I held her close as she rocked again, caught between us, completely filled.

"You were made for this," I whispered. "For us."

She broke on a soft, breathless sound, her body trembling as we began to move together.

And in that moment, with her wrapped around me and him buried behind her, I knew with absolute certainty...

We weren't ever letting her go.

"You're doing so fucking good, baby," Gerasimou grunted behind her, his hips grinding into her ass with slow, heavy thrusts. "You're taking us so goddamn deep."

I slid one hand to her stomach again, palm pressed to that soft skin just below her navel.

"You feel that?" I said, my voice low. "That's me inside you. Right here. Deep. Where I belong."

She let out a broken moan, her body locking up for a second like she didn't know whether to breathe or come.

"Keep going, *Yume*," I whispered, brushing her damp hair from her face. "Don't stop. You're almost there."

"You're dripping," G growled, picking up speed. "Fucking soaked. You feel it? She's leaking down your balls, Carter."

I did.

Her slick coated everything. Every thrust sent a fresh rush between her thighs. She was squirming now, overwhelmed, but unable to stop.

"Fuck...you're close," I said. "I can feel it. You're squeezing me like you're about to come."

"Yeah, you are," G echoed, deeper, nastier. "That ass is clenching so fucking tight. You gonna let go for us? Gonna cum while we're both buried in you?"

She choked on a sob—high and desperate—and rocked her hips again, harder now, chasing it.

"We got you," I told her, kissing her swollen lips from her gnawing on them. "You're safe. Let it happen."

"You gonna explode, baby?" G rasped. "Gods, she's fucking trembling."

And she was.

Her whole body shook. Sweat slick on her back, her thighs soaked, her hands clutching at anything she could reach. Her eyes were glassy, mouth open, panting.

"Cum for us," I said, also picking up speed. "Right here. Just like this."

"Give it to us, baby," G said, his thrusts turning rougher. "Let us feel it. Rain down on us."

Then she broke.

Her scream tore out of her chest—raw and wordless. Her body convulsed between us, her pussy squeezing so hard I nearly lost control. She squirted again, soaking my stomach, drenching us both as her orgasm hit like a wave.

"Fuck, look at her..." G growled, and I felt his pace stutter. "She's milking me...gods—"

I felt her ass clamp down on him just as she screamed again, louder this time. A full-body release, shaking her to the core.

G pulled out quickly and cleaned himself before he eased into her quivering pussy, while I still sat nestled inside.

We gave her a moment to adjust before fucking her. Hard.

Her whole body was quaking, tears falling now, mouth slack, skin flushed all over.

I couldn't hold back anymore.

I gripped her neck, sitting her up some, pushing us deeper inside of her. It wasn't long before heat rushed through me, pouring into her at the same time G did as she trembled around us, her body refusing to stop pulsing.

I held her through it, kissed her shoulder, and ran my fingers over her stomach, right where I hoped my seed would take root.

"You're everything," I whispered.

Behind her, G's forehead dropped to her back, his breath hot and ragged.

We stayed like that for a long moment.

All three of us tangled together.

Everything was the way it should be, finally.

Loralei

You would think after cumming multiple times back-to-back, one would be exhausted. But I wasn't. Was I spent? Sure, but more than anything, my body felt so alive.

It might have also been my fear that if I closed my eyes, when I woke up again, they would be gone.

Before them, I never had to feel the crippling fear of abandonment. Now, I was constantly holding people at arm's length afraid that they would just up and leave me.

Such a silly thought or concept to develop at my age, but when you found something that felt made for your soul like Carter and Gerasimou felt for mine, losing that feeling felt like a part of you was always missing.

"You're thinking too hard, baby," Carter said as he kissed my forehead.

"Yes," Gerasimou cosigned. "Rest, *Lykáki*, we aren't going anywhere. Promise."

Even though just those words eased the fear, I was still wide awake. After we came that last time, I was so spent at first, I didn't even pay attention to anything as they took me to handle my hygiene and changed the bedding.

However, now something in this room felt both different from the room we'd been sharing since we moved into the farmhouse, and at the same time, oddly the same.

I sat up quickly and took in my surroundings. When I noticed the familiar fireplace, drapes, and seating area by the window, hell, even down to the color of the walls, I started to crack up.

"You okay?" Carter asked.

Somehow, his honest concern made me laugh harder. These crazy fuckers indeed kidnapped me again and brought me all the way back to the cabin in Colorado.

"This is hilarious!" I said through my laughter. "I guess y'all have really learned what it meant to be parents."

They were both sitting up now looking at me like I was crazy.

"Can this wait a few hours before she starts spiraling?" Gerasimou said flatly. "I need sleep."

"We're not following, *Yume*," Carter spoke slowly, ignoring Gerasimou.

"Here." I waved my hand in the air. "You had to kidnap me to bring me back to the cabin in Colorado in order to fuck me."

A small smile was on both of their faces as they watched me deliriously laugh at something that truly wasn't even humorous.

"Crazy girl, we didn't bring you to Colorado," Gerasimou said, laying back down, pulling me with him.

"Huh?" I asked,confused.

"We aren't in Colorado, *Yume*," Carter confirmed.

"But... this room." I sat up some, balancing myself on my elbows. "It's the exact one you guys had me in."

"It is," Carter stated simply, head tilted, watching me with a look I couldn't quite place.

That didn't help.

My brows furrowed, still half caught in my own laughter. "Wait... what?"

"We had it brought here" he said, like that wasn't a completely insane sentence.

I blinked at him. "What do you mean, you had it brought here?"

Gerasimou grunted beneath me. "Exactly what it sounds like. Years ago, we had it moved to this land. Wanted the memories."

"What memories?" I asked, though I already knew.

"Our first time," Carter said softly. "The cabin."

I sat all the way up now, staring at the walls, the fireplace, the fucking curtain tiebacks. It was the same. Not similar. The same.

"You wanted our memories?" I asked, voice hoarse from emotion.

"Don't be dramatic," Gerasimou mumbled. "Of course, we did."

Carter didn't even fight a smile.

"I..." I started to say something smart, something cutting, but I couldn't. My throat caught. My stomach tightened. My fingers curled in the sheets.

They remembered. Every detail.

"You kept it," I said instead. "Like down to the scent. Like pine and cedar wood. That was the first smell I woke up to there."

Carter nodded. "We infused the walls."

"You infused the—what are you, interior designers now?"

"Don't tempt him," Gerasimou muttered, eyes closed. "He'll re-paint the whole house next week."

But I couldn't stop staring at the room.

"You really brought it back," I said again, more to myself this time. "Not just the sex. Not just the setup. You brought it back *then*. What we created there."

"We never lost it," Carter said, shifting up behind me, arms wrapping around my waist. "We just... paused it. Grew around it. And now we get to have both. Then and now. Us."

"And this time," Gerasimou added, pulling me back against his chest, "you don't have to wake up alone."

I laid there, sandwiched between them, surrounded by a memory made real.

For a long time, no one said anything.

Then Carter spoke again, lips against my shoulder.

"We aren't leaving again, Yume."

He said it like it was a truth I needed to believe. Like the part of me that laughed too hard at what hurt, that made jokes when I was scared, that looked for exits even in the safest places—was still lovable. Still worth building whole rooms around.

I swallowed. My eyes burned. But I didn't cry.

Instead, I reached for both of them, pulled their hands over my stomach, and closed my eyes.

"I'm not sleeping," I whispered.

"That's fine," Gerasimou murmured, already half gone. "Just don't move."

"I won't," I said.

"Wait." I sat up, and Gerasimou groaned. "One more thing."

"What, *Lykáki*?" he asked, annoyed.

"What land did y'all bring it to? How far are we from the twins?" I asked, my anxiety kicking being too far from the twins.

"Like four hundred feet... maybe," Carter answered, eyes closed.

"Huh?"

"Gods, *Lykáki*," If I wasn't so confused, I would have laughed at how annoyed he was with me. "We moved the cabin on the farmland.

The same house we've been living in sits. Okay, baby? Now for the love of Greece, go to sleep."

"But we rent the farmhouse. Are the owners okay with us putting the cabin here?" I asked.

"Ask yourself that," he said simply.

My eyes ballooned. "Me?"

"*Sí*, when we bought the house, we had it put in your name. We had Fin do all the legal stuff for it. The land is ours, baby."

"You were going to come back for me?"

G looked at me. No smirk. No teasing grin.

"We told you in the letter," he said. "Maybe not directly. But we said we'd come back. That it wasn't the end."

I covered my mouth with one hand. That letter—I still had it. Still kept it folded in a box in my closet, stained and creased from how many times I'd read it in the dark, missing them, not knowing if it had been a promise or a lie.

"And you never moved on?" I whispered.

Carter shook his head. "No. But there was never anyone else. Not really."

"You were ours," Gerasimou said. "You always were."

Tears burned behind my eyes. I swallowed hard, trying to keep them back, but the wave was rising too fast to stop.

"And now?" I asked. "You really think we can just... pick up and build something?"

Carter reached for my hand, lacing our fingers together.

"No," he said. "We don't think. We know."

"But we haven't even spent that much time together," I said, the words tumbling out. "How do we know this will work?"

I desperately needed for us to work.

"We know that," he said gently. "But love doesn't need a countdown. It doesn't require timelines or guarantees."

G leaned in closer, kissing my bare shoulder. "You've always been ours, *Lykáki*. We were just waiting for the world to get quiet enough to say it out loud."

And there it was.

The dam cracked.

Tears spilled, hot and fast, and I didn't even try to hide them. I buried my face in Carter's chest, my hands gripping his arms as the sobs came harder than I expected.

They held me through it. Let me cry without flinching. Didn't rush me. Didn't fix it. Just stayed.

When I finally pulled back, sniffing, breath unsteady, I whispered, "I love you. Both of you. I know it seems crazy or too soon, but I do. I have ever since back in that cabin."

"You didn't have to say it," Carter murmured, brushing a tear from my cheek. "But I'm glad you did."

"We love you too," G said, dragging me into his arms like I weighed nothing. "Even when you're a pain in my ass."

I laughed through my tears, half-sobbing, half-choking. "This is insane."

"It's us," Carter said. "It was always going to be a bit unconventional."

We laid there like that, all three of us tangled in sweat and warmth and the slow settling of something we'd all been chasing for years.

"Can I be honest?" I asked, pulling the blanket up.

"Always," G said.

"I feel... lit."

They both looked at me like I'd started speaking in tongues.

"Lit?" Carter echoed.

"Like..." I stared at the ceiling. "Like something in me just turned on. That flicker that went out when you left? It's back. And I'm terrified, but I'm also... excited. I don't know what our life looks like. But I want it."

"You'll have it," Carter promised. "Whatever you imagine. We'll build it."

"Yeah," G added, voice already dipping with exhaustion again. "And if anyone tries to get in the way this time, we'll bury 'em under the chicken coop."

I burst out laughing. "So romantic."

He shrugged. "We're building a farmhouse life. Shovels are implied."

I curled between them again, smiling into Carter's chest, one hand stretched back to touch G's ribs.

For the first time in years, I didn't feel like I was waiting for the other shoe to drop. I wasn't on edge. I wasn't bracing for heartbreak.

I felt wanted.

Safe.

Chosen.

And maybe this life wouldn't be perfect. Maybe we'd still fight, still stumble. But I was done letting fear write the ending.

I was ready.

For all of it.

For the life we'd build together.

Epilogue

Loralei

"Are we almost there?" I asked the guys.

They had me blindfolded, leading me by the hands. My boots brushed against gravel and cool soil, the air crisp and quiet around us. Somewhere far off, I heard birdsong—soft, distant.

"It's not far," Carter said, gently tightening his grip on mine.

"'Not far' better not mean a half-mile uphill," I muttered.

"You'll live," Gerasimou said.

I exhaled through a smile. It was my birthday. They'd already gone all out. A slow morning with the twins, gifts they'd helped pick, glitter stuck to my palms from hand-drawn cards. Carter had made breakfast. G had cleaned up. I'd been kissed senseless and pampered like they had nowhere else in the world to be.

Then Jessie and Julie had shown up just after lunch. Their timing was too perfect. Matching smiles. Matching excuses.

"We'll stay with the twins tonight," Julie had said. "Don't argue."

Jessie winked. "It's handled."

I should've known something was coming.

Now here I was, blindfolded again, surrounded by the smell of earth and something sterile beneath it.

We stopped.

"You ready?" Carter asked behind me.

I nodded.

Gerasimou pulled the blindfold off.

I blinked into the yellowed lighting—dim, humming, too far underground for comfort. Concrete walls. Cold. The space smelled like old blood and metal. A single chair sat bolted to the floor, chains wrapped tight. A drain carved beneath it. The silence was loud.

And in that chair, head up, face battered but smirking?

Javier.

Even after all this time, months since Berlin, months since the night I should've killed him. He still managed to look smug. His body had clearly been handled. His face wore healing cuts, stitches, swelling that hadn't fully faded. But his mouth? Still curved like he thought he'd won something.

"Well," he rasped, voice wrecked but still that thick accented smugness. "Look what the birthday girl bought herself."

I didn't say a word. Didn't care he knew it was my birthday.

I stepped forward, slow and calm.

"She finally come to thank me?" he asked, addressing the room. "I mean, if it weren't for me, you three wouldn't be playing house with your lies and half-truths."

Carter didn't move.

Gerasimou stood with his arms crossed.

Javier's smile widened. "No 'thank you'? Not even a little gratitude for bringing you putas together?"

Still, I didn't speak.

He leaned forward as far as the chains allowed, which wasn't much. "You don't even know how close I came. You think I took them to just sell? No, *quierda*. I took them to send a message."

My breath stilled.

"I had buyers lined up. A girl and a boy, untraceable, healthy, mixed lineage—premium value. The girl would've gone first. They always go first. The boy... maybe he'd have made it longer. Or maybe they'd have kept them together for the novelty."

The air left my lungs.

Carter's jaw clenched. I could hear it crack.

G's hands were balled at his sides.

But me?

I stepped forward until I could see every line of that grotesque smile. Every fracture in the healing bone. The blood at the corner of his mouth from where he'd probably reopened something, trying to laugh.

"You took my children," I said, voice low. "You planned to sell them like livestock."

He shrugged. "Don't act so sanctimonious. People do worse every day."

A gun was placed in my hand.

His eyes dropped to it, then came back to mine. "You're really going to waste your birthday wish on me?"

"You think this is a waste?" I asked.

He said nothing.

"I didn't kill you in Berlin because you were useful. They wanted your contacts, your network, your mouth still moving."

I stepped closer.

"But you're not useful anymore."

He swallowed. First sign of fear. Like he truly didn't think I would do it.

"Oh, so the whore can fight her own battles," Javier mocked, using it as a shield to hide his fear. "Here I thought you let them fight your battles for you."

I tilted my head. "You think I won't do it?"

"No, I thought you'd scream. Curse. Tell me how I broke you."

"You didn't break me," I said. "You tried and failed, but I will thank you because without your attempt, I wouldn't have gotten them back. Carter wouldn't have his mother, his sisters. And while you rot in the fucking ground like the worm you are, I will be getting my back blown. Like your head."

And I shot him.

Once.

Right between the eyes.

He dropped back into the chair like a puppet whose strings had been cut. Blood trailed slowly down his temple, a single thread painting the side of his face. He didn't twitch. He didn't speak again.

Silence swallowed the space.

I let the gun fall to my side, breathing steady.

I didn't cry.

Didn't collapse.

It wasn't revenge.

It was correction.

Carter stepped up beside me, wrapping an arm gently around my waist. Gerasimou came to my other side, placing his hand on the top of my head pulling me closer into him, kissing the top of it.

Neither of them said anything.

They didn't need to.

When we stepped back outside, the air was fresh again, birds still singing. Spring green at the edges of the trees, defiant in its softness.

I looked up at the pale sky and exhaled.

There was no more chase.

No lingering threat.

No more wondering what would come back to haunt me.

Only the life we were building on the land they bought for me. For us.

Back at the house, our twins would be curled up with their aunts, giggling at stories, demanding snacks they didn't need.

And tomorrow, we'd wake up and keep building.

Not out of survival.

Out of choice.

"I'm ready," I said.

Carter kissed the side of my head. "Then let's go home."

Gerasimou grunted. "Next year, we're doing cake."

I smiled. No longer looking back, but forward.

A Few Words

To my kids and Husband I love you. To my sisters thank you for being just there always. My BesLie girl you already know how it goes love you! Nasa truly thank you for all the late night convos and reading this over for me.

Thank you immensely to my readers for going through t this throuples journey and i am so grateful for your buying or downloading this book.

Alright I'm done but you'll see these three again in Deidre and Cyrus's book. and booooooooyyy they are going to be a time... Thank y'all for reading!

Don't forget to come join my FB reading group and my socials

https://www.facebook.com/groups/tashiebabies

IG: https://www.instagram.com/tashtheauthor

TikTok: https://www.tiktok.com/@tashtheauthor

xoxo Tash